CONTAMINATION

BOOK ZERO

BY T. W. PIPERBROOK

ABOUT CONTAMINATION: ZERO

The infection starts with Frank, one of the locals at the town bar. In just a few hours, it has consumed the entire town.

Dan Lowery, one of only four police officers in St. Matthews, soon realizes he is no match for the impending destruction. Violence and bloodshed litter the streets, and the infected roam freely. No one is safe here — not even his family.

Somewhere, someone knows what is happening, and about the horrors to come...but is it too late?

SERIES PREQUEL. 92 PAGES.

CONTAMINATION PREQUEL
CONTAMINATION 1: THE ONSET
CONTAMINATION 2: CROSSROADS
CONTAMINATION 3: WASTELAND
CONTAMINATION 4: ESCAPE
CONTAMINATION 5: SURVIVAL
CONTAMINATION 6: SANCTUARY

Want to know when the next book is coming out?
Sign up for NEW RELEASE ALERTS
and get a FREE STORY!
http://eepurl.com/qy_SH

EPITAPH

*To those we have loved, those we have
lost, and those we hold onto.
In Loving Memory JAD 1922 – 2012*

PART ONE
THE LAST SUPPER

1

THE PRISONER LUNGED THROUGH THE bars and grabbed hold of Dan Lowery's collar.

"When I get out of here, this game is over!" he shrieked, eyes bloodshot and bulging.

Dan reached for his holster, but thought better of it. He wrenched his shirt free instead, and leapt back a few feet. He cursed himself silently for getting too close to the cell. The prisoner glared at him, jaw hanging open, his pupils wide and distorted. His speech was slurred, and his breath reeked of another night wasted at the bar. His bald head captured the bright lights of the jail cell, reflecting the glare back off his scalp.

Dan fingered the badge on his chest and lifted it up so the prisoner could see. "You pull that shit again, and I'll have you charged with assaulting a police officer. You hear me, Frank?"

Frank wasn't listening. He was busy pacing around the cell, and had probably already forgotten what had just transpired. He clutched his stomach and bent over the cell bench, dry heaving.

Dan unfolded his sleeves. He had rolled them up prior to transporting the man from cruiser to cell. There was always a fight to be had with this one, and he was getting damn tired of it.

This time, it had been a dispute over the television station at The Down Under. Frank had insisted the barkeep change the channel so he could watch the boxing match. One of the other locals had resisted, claiming he wanted to catch the weather first. A verbal altercation had ensued, culminating in Frank tripping over his barstool and landing flat on his back. He had screamed and ranted, and had finally been detained by several other patrons. Dan had arrived shortly after, dodging the man's vomit as he hauled him into the back of the cruiser.

This wasn't the life he had envisioned when joining the police force. At the same time, he wasn't sure what more to expect from a small town in Arizona. With a population of only a few thousand, St. Matthews had little room in the budget for reinforcements. Dan was one of only four police officers.

He moved through the small station, heading towards a locker room down the hall from the jail cell. He could still hear Frank coughing and spewing behind him.

"You'd think you would have learned your lesson by now, Frank," he mumbled.

"Fuck you!" the man screamed from the other

room. Dan had forgotten how sound carried in the hollow building.

He entered the locker room, already unbuttoning his shirt. It had been a long day, and he was ready to knock off for the evening. Officer Howard Barrett was already suiting up, ready to relieve him of his duties. Howard was the station's senior officer.

"You mean I have to watch this joker all night? What the fuck, man?" Howard rolled his eyes, suppressing a laugh.

"Better you than me!" Dan retorted, hanging his shirt in his locker.

The dispatcher had already left for the day. After hours, all calls were routed through a regional office in a neighboring town. Howard would be alone with the prisoner for the rest of the evening.

Howard buttoned his uniform over his chest, covering a scar on his left shoulder. Howard was originally from California. In his eight years of service on the Sacramento streets, the officer had been shot twice, each time refusing desk duty. The scar was one of two on his body—the other was on his calf. Dan had seen them plenty of times. His comrade took pleasure in reliving the stories, showing his wounds with pride to anyone who would listen.

It was a far cry from herding the local drunks into a cell for the evening.

"So what's Julie got on the burner for you?"

"Word on the street is ham and boiled potatoes." Dan smiled. Oftentimes, he would invite Howard over to join them when they both had the night off.

"Ah, an Irish feast! Well, enjoy it man. I'm sure I won't feel like eating much after watching Frank throw up in there."

Howard slammed the locker shut, and the door rattled through the small room. Although he was only five foot nine, he had the build of a football player, making up for his lack of height with a thick, rugged frame.

"I'll see you tomorrow," Dan said.

From the other room, Frank continued to dry heave, and Dan chuckled softly.

"Good luck with that one."

Dan walked across the parking lot, feeling the cool breeze ruffle through his curly blonde hair. His face reddened as the Arizona heat hit his pores. He wiped his arm across his face and felt the perspiration moisten his skin.

He was exhausted. After a long day at work, he was looking forward to spending time with his wife and daughter. On a typical day, they would bring out some of the board games they had tucked in the closet, or enjoy a relaxing walk in the yard. He hoped today was no different.

He looked down at his cellphone, preparing

for it to ring at any minute. Julie was punctual, and she'd be expecting him shortly. Within a few seconds, the phone lit up. He laughed to himself.

"Hello?"

"What's so funny?" Julie demanded, but he could hear that she was in a good mood.

"Nothing, honey. I just knew you'd be calling. Right on time, as usual!" he kidded, reaching for his car keys.

"I've got your favorite meal on the stove. Quinn even helped with the potatoes."

"I can't wait! I'll be there shortly."

"I love you," she said.

Dan hung up and inserted his key in the car door. The police vehicle was a 2006 Ford Crown Victoria. Given the size of St. Matthews, the town's officers normally used their patrol cars as their primary mode of transportation. In the event of an emergency, they would be expected to spring into action at a moment's notice.

Dan had rarely been required to do so. He kept his radio by the bedside table, just in case, but he couldn't remember the last time it had woken him from sleep.

He often caught Julie staring at it before going to bed. He imagined she was having a silent chat with the device, warning it to stay silent.

Dan pulled out of the lot and into the roadway. He lived within 3 miles of the station, which provided a quick commute from work to home. Because of this, he used the time to unwind – to transition from his rugged exterior as a police officer into his role as father and husband.

He loved his position on the force, but Julie and Quinn were his main focus—the reason he woke up in the morning.

Dan navigated the streets with ease. It hadn't taken him long to gain familiarity with St. Matthews. In fact, there weren't many streets that he didn't know. The city roads were well maintained, featuring a mixture of commercial and residential properties. In between them, small shrubs peppered the dusty landscape, constant reminders of the desert backdrop.

The White Mountains surrounded the town on all sides. A frequent destination for Arizona tourists, they provided a makeshift border, sheltering St. Matthews from the neighboring towns and insulating them from the worries of big city life.

Dan rounded a corner, heading away from the center of town and into one of the residential neighborhoods. Here, houses dominated the roadside, and he relaxed slightly. He was a few blocks from home when his cellphone rang.

He glanced at the display, expecting to see his wife's name. Instead, he saw Howard's.

"Hey, man. Want me to save you a plate of potatoes?" He grinned.

"Dan?" Howard's voice wavered.

For a split second, it sounded like the reception

had been lost. A deep breath from the other end told him that his friend was still on the line.

"Are you still there?" Dan asked.

"Frank's dead."

The words rang in the air. Dan stared at the phone in disbelief.

"What happened?"

"Can you come back to the station?" Howard begged.

In his five years on the force, it was the first time Dan had heard his friend rattled.

"I'll be right there," he said, closing the phone.

He threw on his sirens and raced back into town.

2

HOWARD MET HIM AT THE station door. The front of his shirt was covered in sweat, and he looked visibly upset. His usually stocky frame seemed to be shrunken, as if he were trying to disappear into his clothes.

"Are you ok?" Dan asked.

"I think so," Howard said, but his demeanor said otherwise.

"Where is he?"

"In the cell. I covered him with a blanket. I called the paramedics, but it sounded like they'd be a while."

Dan was hit by a pang of fear, but he wasn't sure why. His friend was making him nervous. He hurried through the door and down the hall to where Frank had been kept. As he proceeded, he half-expected to hear the prisoner still cursing, spilling the contents of his stomach onto the jail floor.

Instead, the station was eerily quiet.

Howard hung behind him, as if afraid of what his friend might find.

"I've never seen anything like this," he said.

Dan entered the main room, feeling his heartbeat quicken in his chest. In the center of the cell, a bulky figure was covered in a blue blanket. For a second, he imagined that Frank was hiding somewhere in the station; that the lump under the blanket was a decoy, and that the prisoner would come lunging at them from the shadows.

Pull yourself together, he thought.

He tugged on the cell door, but it was locked. He reached for his keys.

He stopped when he noticed a trickle of dried blood on one of the iron bars. The fluid had made its way down the side of the cell, forming a pool at the bottom.

"What the fuck?" He stepped back.

"He attacked me, Dan. I was lucky to get out of the room alive."

Howard motioned towards his arm. The officer's shirt was torn at the elbow, and a red stain blossomed towards his bicep. Dan was surprised he hadn't noticed it before.

"Howard, you're hurt! What the hell happened?"

"He took a chunk out of my arm, man. I thought he was going to rip it off." Howard covered his face with his good hand.

Dan drew his gun. He inserted the key into the lock, watching for any sign of movement through the bars, his finger on the trigger of the pistol. The blanket remained still on the floor.

"Stay back," he warned, stepping inside.

Dan crossed the cell towards the body, and immediately gagged. A puddle of Frank's vomit lay under the steel bench. If circumstances were different, he might have found it amusing.

He nudged the blanket with his foot, expecting Frank to grab onto it in a drunken rage. The figure remained stiff. He bent down slowly, grabbing the edge of the fabric, and slid it off a few inches. It dragged slightly, caught on a piece of flesh that looked like the prisoner's ear.

Dan recoiled in fear. Frank's face was demolished: his bare head was split open at the center. His shiny round head had become a red canvas, painted with a mural of blood and exposed bone. His nose was splintered into fragments, and his mouth dangled open, held together by a few pieces of teeth and loose gum. His eyes were rolled up into his head. They were pitch black.

"He was reaching for the water cooler. It looked like he was thirsty. I went to give him a cup—you know, to be nice." Howard eyed his friend, as if afraid he wouldn't believe him. "And then he grabbed me, man! When I broke free, he went crazy. He kept smashing his head against the bars, over and over, trying to get to me, until his face just...oh Jesus fuck!"

Howard shook his head from side to side, trying to keep his composure. The senior officer had been shot twice—and had survived some of the toughest neighborhoods in California—but tonight he had finally cracked.

"Did you see his eyes?" Howard waved his good arm towards the cell. "What the fuck could have happened to him?"

Dan replaced the blanket, feeling his stomach tighten. He stepped back, bumping into an object on the floor. A plastic cup rolled away from him and came to rest underneath the bench.

In his five years on the force, this was one of the most violent deaths he had ever seen. Dan was worried.

Mickey Sonstrom arrived on the scene first, even before the ambulance. He was fair-skinned and freckled, sporting a tuft of red hair that crept out from underneath his police hat. His chin pointed outwards, as if to constantly reaffirm his position of authority. At twenty-two, he was the youngest officer on the force.

"Howard, what'd you do, man?" he kidded, punching the stocky officer on the arm. "Oh shit, man, I didn't know you were hurt. Are you all right?"

"It's not funny, Mickey," Dan scolded him. "Howard is lucky to be alive."

"Is Frank really dead?"

"Yes, he is. We should wait for Sheriff Turner before we do anything."

The red-haired officer peered over their shoulders into the cell, catching a glimpse of the blue blanket. Dan had placed it back over the body, both to preserve the evidence and to avoid looking at it again. Over the past few years, there had been a few gruesome deaths in St. Matthews, but nothing to this extent.

Mickey headed off into the locker room.

"I'll get the camera," he said.

Howard sat behind the wooden desk in the room, applying pressure to his wound. They had raided the emergency kit in the station and wrapped his arm with gauze and a bandage while waiting for the paramedics. Dan was sure the man would need stitches.

Frank had sliced into a piece of the man's upper bicep, presumably with his nails. Dan struggled to figure out how the prisoner had done so much damage — especially without a weapon.

"I should call my wife," Dan said. "She's probably worried."

"Why don't you go home, man? Have dinner with the family," Howard offered.

"Absolutely not. I'll tell her not to wait up."

Dan retrieved his phone and walked into the corridor. The sound of his footsteps bounced off the station walls as he dialed the number. His wife picked up on the first ring.

"Dan, where are you?" Julie said. "I thought you'd be home already."

"We had an accident at the station, honey.

CONTAMINATION: BOOK ZERO

Howard's been hurt. He'll be ok—but there is an incident that I need to deal with."

"Oh my God. I knew it. Will you be home soon?"

"I don't think so," he said. "In fact, I'm pretty sure it will be a while."

"I'll wait up for you. I can heat up dinner when you get back."

Dan smiled, feeling a sense of relief at the sound of her voice. Howard was still alive. Julie and Quinn were safe at home, miles away from the carnage he had just witnessed. Things could be much worse.

"That sounds great. If you guys get hungry, feel free to start without me," he said. Dan doubted he would have much of an appetite.

He hung up the cellphone and stared at his reflection in the glass. His adrenaline was still flowing, and he tried to steady his hands. The ambulance would be here soon, and they would need to assess the crime scene. He tried to regain his composure. From somewhere outside, a car door slammed shut. He slipped the phone back into his pocket and adjusted his hat.

Even before he had a visual, Dan heard his boss breathing from the parking lot outside. A few seconds later, the door swung open with a *crash*, and Sheriff Turner's massive figure filled the entrance. He lumbered down the hall towards Dan, his legs shaking the ground beneath him.

"Is Howard ok?" he asked.

"I think he'll be fine," Dan assured him. "But he'll need stitches."

The Sheriff muttered something and wiped away a stream of sweat from beneath his cap. His short white hair was matted into clumps, and his thick black eyebrows quivered with worry. Labored breaths wracked his body. Dan figured it had probably been a while since the man had moved so fast. By all accounts, his boss was sorely out of shape; however, his intentions were some of the purest that Dan had ever known.

Sheriff Turner had taken over the position from Bill Turner, his father, who had retired after forty years on the force. The family had occupied St. Matthews for generations, each member holding a career in public service. Almost anywhere the sheriff went he was greeted by warmth and respect. He once joked that his body belonged to the townsfolk. Dan thought he should have been a politician in another life.

The sheriff's red cheeks puffed in front of him, and he resumed walking.

"Thank God he's all right," he said. "Where the hell are the medics?"

It was after 9 o'clock when Dan finally left the police station. At that point, there wasn't much more he could do. Howard had been taken to the hospital to be stitched up, insisting that his co-workers stay behind. Dan had completed the necessary paperwork; the three remaining officers had documented the scene.

Frank's mangled body had been taken to the morgue shortly after. The coroner, Jonas Cutler, hadn't offered much of an explanation. Even with an autopsy, he explained, it would be impossible to gauge the man's motives. For now, he was chalking it up to a stomach full of alcohol and a bad temper.

Dan pulled out of the parking lot. He contemplated calling his wife, but given the late hour, he decided against it. In the event his family had gone to sleep, he didn't want to wake them — though he was certain Julie would be up, waiting for him.

As he sped home, he tried to picture the plate of re-heated potatoes and ham that awaited him, but only succeeded in conjuring up images of Frank's missing face. He blinked hard a few times, trying to get a grip on his stomach. Work was work, and home was home. He kept reminding himself of that fact. A few minutes later, he pulled into the driveway.

The Lowery residence was a quaint, single-story home situated on a slightly wooded lot. The front lower half was comprised of red brick, the upper made of white wood panels. Two elm trees sat in the front yard, providing a nice contrast to the desert backdrop. On the right side of the house was a two-car garage.

Dan felt above the visor for the garage remote, and then reconsidered, parking the cruiser where he had pulled in.

He'd leave the garage doors closed, just in case they were asleep.

He exited the vehicle, locked the car door, and started up the walkway. A dim light was on in the dining room. He felt a sense of relief wash over him. It was good to be home.

3

HOWARD WINCED AS THE NURSE threaded the first stitch. The pain was actually quite bearable, but he wasn't a fan of needles. He looked away and concentrated on a diagram on the wall. A row of letters and numbers lined the poster, each varying in size and shape.

"Can you read all of them?" The nurse smiled at him. She was a cute blonde, probably no more than twenty-eight, if he had to guess.

"Let's see, A, F, G. Yep—got 'em all." He grinned, flexing his bicep.

"You'll have to stay still, sir."

"No problem, ma'am," he said.

Howard thought back to the last time he had been in the hospital, back in Sacramento. That was when he had received the gunshot wound to his calf. Now, that was some scary shit. *This is nothing*, he reminded himself. *Nothing at all.*

He should've known better than to go near Frank's cell. He'd known something was going to happen tonight.

He closed his left eye and tried reading the

letters on the chart backwards. He realized that the patients who took the test were probably farther away, but it felt good to practice nonetheless. Howard was on a constant quest for perfection, always striving to keep his mind and body active.

He closed both eyes as the needle wove in and out of his arm. He could feel a steady pinching even though he had been given an anesthetic. He pictured his arm slowly coming back together, and tried to dispel the image of Frank's face coming apart.

"All set!" the nurse said, standing up proudly.

Howard wondered how many times she had given stitches before. From the look in her eyes, she was quite impressed with the work she had done.

"Looks good!" he confirmed, but figured he wouldn't have known the difference either way.

The nurse beamed and put away her supplies.

"Hey, if you ever get bored, I work at the precinct downtown," he said. "You should stop by. Ask for Howard."

"Definitely!" She smiled, but her blue eyes remained on the equipment. A few seconds later, she handed him a sheet of paper. "All of your post-care instructions are listed here on the bottom. We'll see you in two weeks to remove the stitches."

Howard thanked her and slid off the chair. He retrieved his cap from the table, and exited into the hallway.

The emergency room waiting area was surprisingly quiet. Two rows of red plastic chairs lined the walls, all of them empty but for a few magazines that had been left on the seats. Behind the front desk, an older woman sat with her back to the room, scribbling away on some paperwork.

A television hung from the ceiling, displaying the local newscast. The sound was barely audible, but Howard could make out the story from the tagline below. The reporter was covering the town's yearly festival. Several residents had planted a variety of trees on the center green. The caption switched a few seconds later to an alert on a recall of ground beef.

"I could go for a burger," he mumbled to himself, wishing he were hungry.

He exited through the automatic doors and back into the night.

Howard drove aimlessly for a few hours, rounding the streets of St. Matthews in the police cruiser. He should probably go home, but home felt like the wrong place to be. For a second, he considered calling Dan, perhaps stopping in for some ham and potatoes, but thought better of it.

There was no time for that now.

A glimmer of pain rippled up his arm, and he loosened his grip on the steering wheel.

For a Friday night, the streets were unusually

empty. Normally, he would find himself stuck behind some drunk who was driving far less than the speed limit, painfully aware of the cruiser behind him. Tonight, he was greeted by nothing more than the traffic lights and an occasional foot traveler.

Howard circled the town several times before he realized where he was headed. He pulled into a small side street tucked in the commercial center of town and turned off his headlights. A row of brick buildings loomed overhead, the adobe cracked and worn from both time and lack of concern. A few patrons were standing in the alleyway, but quickly dispersed when they saw the patrol car. Howard noticed that one of them pointed in his direction. It looked like the man had mouthed the officer's name.

Above them, a dingy sign garnished one of the doorways, adding a faint orange glow to the alley. Howard looked up at it. *The Down Under*.

Normally, a trip to the bar would have been under the pretext of violence—an alcohol-fueled fight, a gun scare, or perhaps a drug overdose. Tonight, he had been drawn to the place for another reason.

On any given night, Frank would have still been here, raising his glass to anything that struck his fancy, and raising his fists at everything else. Howard closed his eyes, breathing in the smell of warm beer and stale urine. If he listened intently enough, he was almost certain he could hear the dead man's voice, yelling from inside.

After a few minutes, he opened his eyes and stared out the window. A few of the locals had gathered in front of the bar and were pointing and whispering at him. He sat upright, instinctively feeling for his pistol.

One of them held a bottle in his hand and staggered a few steps toward the vehicle. Howard recognized him as one of the locals—Nathan Heid. "What's the matter, you pigs come to arrest another one of us? One man isn't enough for the night? You fucking assholes."

Howard winced at the insult. He could easily arrest the man on several charges, but tonight he had much more important things to do. Nathan leered at him, preening a scruffy white beard. "Yeah, that's right. You got nothin' to say now, huh?"

The others cheered, laughing and holding up their bottles.

Howard started the engine and put the car into drive, trying his best to appear unfazed. He sped off down the alley, feeling utterly alone.

4

DAN STARTED UP THE WALKWAY, and then stopped. He glanced back at the police cruiser, which was immersed in shadow at the foot of the driveway. The motion light over his garage must have gone out. He cursed silently and walked back towards the vehicle, intending to pull it into the garage. From the looks of it, Julie and Quinn were both still up, so he wouldn't be disturbing them.

He hopped back in the car and tapped the overhead garage remote. The door ascended, and he flicked on his headlights. Inside, a neat array of garden tools hung on the walls — shovels, rakes, pitchforks — along with neatly stacked bags of potting soil and plant fertilizer on the floor. His wife had always had a green thumb. If Dan so much as looked at a plant, it would disintegrate.

He pulled the cruiser into the garage next to his wife's Subaru Outback. It appeared she hadn't been out today. Normally he could tell by the position of the vehicle. From his job on the force, Dan had inherited an eye for detail. He was often expected to recall facts and conversations in his reports, and he prided himself on his accuracy.

Dan turned off the headlights and tapped the garage remote. He heard the door descend behind him, and checked quickly in his rearview to make sure no one had slipped inside. You could never be too careful. Especially after the night he'd just had.

A few months back, he had responded to a burglary call just outside the town center. Apparently, the suspect had waited outside an elderly woman's home, and then followed her inside through the garage. The perpetrator had then bound and gagged her, before making off with all her valuables. The poor woman had been so shaken up that she had moved into a group home shortly afterwards. Dan couldn't blame her. It was a shame what the world had come to.

He exited the vehicle and made his way to the door. He could hear the television from inside. He turned the handle and stepped into the kitchen, expecting Julie to be there, waiting for him. Instead, he was met with silence. He placed his keys on the countertop.

"Julie, I'm home!" he called out.

The kitchen was in disarray. Pots and pans were strewn across the countertop. A cutting board spilled over with potato skins, and wet towels were draped over the edge of the sink. Julie was normally a neat freak, cleaning her dishes almost immediately after she used them. This wasn't like her. His gaze continued down the counter.

The microwave door had been left open, revealing a splattering of food on the inside. A display of knives was turned sideways next to it. One of them — the largest — was missing. Dan started forward and felt his foot hit a roll of paper towels that had unraveled on the floor.

"Julie?"

Through the kitchen, past an arched doorway, he had a partial view of the dining room. Although the chandelier was lit, it cast only a dull aura over the table, as if the dimmer had been placed on the lowest setting. His wife sat at the head of the table at the end closest to him, her back turned.

"You ok? I'm sorry I'm late."

She didn't answer. Dan's heart hammered behind his ribcage, and his police instincts kicked into gear. He imagined the worst — that someone was waiting for him on the other side of the dining room, forcing his wife to remain silent. From his position, he could only see half of the table. Quinn was nowhere in sight.

His fingertips grazed the gun, but he didn't remove it. Not yet.

He crept past the refrigerator, hugging the side of the room. Slowly, the dining room revealed itself to him. The other chairs were empty; the table was set for three. A whiff of steam rose from the plate in front of Julie, indicating that she had recently heated the food. She was alone.

"Honey, did Quinn go to bed already?" he whispered.

Her neck twitched slightly at the words, and he could see her chest rise and fall. Whatever had happened—*was* happening—she was alive.

He weaved around her chair until her face came into view, still fingering his holster. Her long brown hair was tied in a ponytail, but several strands had made their way out of the elastic and across her face. Her round lips were pursed, and her high cheeks held a faint red glow. Her eyes were closed, and her hands were folded in her lap.

"Are you asleep?"

The TV blared from the other room, but his wife did not make a sound. A few bites were missing from the plate in front of her. The fork was on the floor by her feet.

"Honey..." he tried again, softly.

A *bang* erupted from down the hall. Dan jumped and withdrew his gun. There were two doors beyond the dining room, one on either side. The one on the left was open, and he could see their queen-size bed through the crack. The door across the hall—the one leading to Quinn's bedroom—was shut.

Dan edged sideways down the hallway, keeping one eye on his wife. From the other room, the TV went to commercial, increasing in volume. An announcer spoke of the revolutionary power of a new toilet spray. The rest of the house maintained its silence.

He reached the door and pressed his ear against it. A thin scratching sound emanated from the other side, a few feet below his head. It was about where his daughter's shoulders would be.

He cupped one hand to the door. "Quinn...are you in there?"

Boom! The door wobbled as something crashed against it, knocking his hand from the frame. Someone pounded on the other side, and he heard the person whimpering. It sounded like his daughter, but he couldn't be sure. Dan held the doorknob, turning it slightly to test it. The door was locked. He looked down at the keyhole, but no key was present. It had been locked from the hallway.

His eyes darted back to the dining room table. His wife had not moved, but her eyes were now open. She stared at him vacantly, her lips still pursed together. Her eyes had turned black.

Something glimmered from the table, next to her plate. It was the key to his daughter's room.

Dan made a lunge for the key, and then stopped short. His wife sat motionless, piercing him with hollow eyes. He wondered if she was able to see him—to recognize the man standing before her. Everything about her was horribly wrong.

"Julie, our daughter is locked in her room. We need to get her out," he said. "Do you hear me?"

Her hands remained in her lap, and when he looked down, he could just make out the shiny blade of the kitchen knife. She didn't answer him. What the hell was going on?

Dan reached for the key, closed his hand around it. In the background, the banging had increased in volume, echoing through the hallway and drowning out the TV.

"Quinn, honey, I'm coming!" he shouted behind him.

Julie's hand flew up suddenly, clutching the knife, and she rammed it down, lodging the blade deep in the tabletop. Dan withdrew his hand, but the tip of the blade caught on one of his knuckles, tearing it open. The key clattered to the floor.

"Julie—it's me!" he screamed in pain, watching a crease open in his skin. Blood oozed from his finger. He reached for his handcuffs, hoping to restrain her, but he'd already changed his clothes at the station, and he'd left them in the car.

He jumped back, aiming his pistol at her. Julie had risen to her feet. She wore a mid-length white sundress, and she held the blade to her chest against it. Dan watched a splotch of blood—*his blood*—expand and stain the fabric.

She walked toward him, her chest butting up against the pistol, and raised the knife in the air for another blow. He batted at it with the gun, connecting with the steel blade, but she kept her grip.

Then, before he could react, Julie leapt forward

and sliced. Dan fell backwards, his wife on top of him.

He grabbed hold of her wrist, catching knife and arm at bay, and looked into her face, hoping she would recognize him. Her cheeks were red with blush, the color evenly applied on both sides. Whatever had happened to her, it must have been recent. *I just talked to her a few hours earlier, for God's sake,* he thought. Her eyes were black ovals, penetrating past Dan and etching invisible holes into the floor.

In the background, the banging had lessened. He wondered if Julie had locked their daughter in her own room for her own protection, before the violent urges had taken her over—to stop from killing her own daughter.

"Julie, please stop this," he pleaded.

Her mouth opened, and he noticed bits of food were stuck in her teeth, as if she'd forgotten how to chew. She pushed harder, grunting as she leaned into the knife. It was the first sound she had made since his arrival.

Somewhere in his pocket, Dan's cellphone rang. He blinked away his tears and tried to stop his wife from stabbing him.

5

HOWARD DROVE AIMLESSLY, TRYING TO lose himself in the streets of St. Matthews. He rolled down the window, letting the cool mountain breeze seep into the vehicle, and contemplated having a cigarette.

Howard hadn't smoked in almost ten years. In his twenties, he had maintained a solid pack-a-day habit, lighting up whenever the desire struck him. At the time, he had little concern for the future. He'd been in college then, and life was as simple as passing a few courses at Sacramento State University—just enough to keep him enrolled. At night his real life began: hitting the bars with his friends, playing pool, and chasing the young women that matriculated at the local college. Things had changed rapidly when his mother had fallen ill.

Howard had been home for a visit when she had told him. The doctors had diagnosed her with lung cancer. According to the test results, the disease was already in the advanced stages. She'd been coughing up blood for several weeks before going to the doctor, and a CAT scan had revealed the news. She hadn't even been a smoker. Howard was devastated.

For the next two years, he watched her deteriorate rapidly, losing the strength to walk and eventually becoming bed-ridden. Howard had dropped out of school to take care of her, working nightshifts to assist her during the day. His days were spent at chemotherapy and doctor visits, and he struggled to pay the mortgage and other bills that kept them in the house.

As quickly as the disease had descended upon her, it was gone. His mother passed away in her sleep, only two years after being diagnosed. She was forty-six. Her passing had left him feeling angry and alone.

After her death, Howard joined the police force, throwing his aggression into intense physical training. He shunned his previous lifestyle of drinking and smoking and aimed for a life of clarity and focus. He pushed his body to its limits, fearing that if he let up, he would be overtaken by sickness.

Now, in the wake of the evening's events, he found himself clamoring for a taste of his past. *A cigarette would taste damn good right about now*, he thought.

But that would be a sign of weakness, and one the Agents wouldn't allow.

In the distance, he could make out the White Mountains spiraling upwards into the heavens, oblivious to the concerns of the townspeople below. He sighed and placed his police hat on the seat next to him. He should probably be getting home.

Howard's pocket vibrated, and he jumped to attention. He reached for his cellphone, expecting to see the number of the sheriff, who would be calling to check up on him. His boss had instructed him to take a few weeks off—to heal and unwind from the trauma of the evening. Maybe the man missed him already.

It wasn't Sheriff Turner. It was Dan.

"Hello?"

The cellphone hissed and crackled in response. Howard smiled, wondering if his co-worker had placed the call by accident. He listened for a few seconds, just in case.

"Dan, you there?"

A *crash* erupted through the phone, and he held his ear away from the receiver to soften the noise. He heard the sound of heavy breathing, as if someone was winded.

Or perhaps engaged in a struggle.

Howard strained to hear through the static. His heart galloped as a voice cut through the line.

"*Please stop...*" the person begged. The voice was Dan's.

Howard was only a few minutes from Dan's

house. He paused for a minute, then threw on his sirens, watching the yellows and reds pulse on the road in front of him. He grabbed his radio with his right arm and felt his wounded arm bend below the bandage. He winced and pushed the button.

"All available units, this is Officer Barrett. I'm heading to a possible 240 at 5 Shunpike Place. Need backup ASAP."

He released the lever and waited, rounding the next corner and nearly hitting the curb. Mickey's voice cut through the silence, back at him.

"Howard? Aren't you supposed to be at home resting?"

"I was. I'm heading to Dan's house now. I think he's in trouble."

"I'm on my way," the kid responded. *"I'm across town. Give me a few."*

The cruiser bounded forward, Howard's thoughts with it. He thought of Frank's former comrades from The Down Under, raising their bottles in defiance at him. The world was full of scum. In his earlier years, he would have arrested them without question. But he knew now that it was useless. The next morning, they'd be out on the streets doing the same things.

People rarely changed.

He looked down at the cellphone in his lap, but it remained silent. He was almost to Dan's.

A few minutes later, he pulled onto Shunpike Place and approached the Lowery residence. The driveway was empty, but several lights blazed from inside. Normally, Dan and Julie parked their cars in the garage, so there was a good chance they were at home.

Howard exited the vehicle, drawing his gun with his bad arm. It was still numb from the anesthesia, and he wondered if he could even shoot.

He'd been careless in getting too close to Frank.

He wouldn't make that same mistake again.

He crept towards the house on the paved walkway. Through the front windows, the living room appeared empty. To the right of the living room, he could make out the dining room, which was dimly lit. It appeared that the family had been in the process of eating dinner. He saw plates of food on the table, and glasses that were filled with liquid. Strangely, nobody was there to enjoy it.

Howard approached the windows for a better look. The chair at the head of the table had been knocked backwards, splintering on the dining room floor below. A glimmer of movement next to it drew his attention.

A figure was kneeling on the ground, one thin arm outstretched high into the air. A cascade of long brown hair covered the person's face, obscuring a positive identification, but it looked like a female.

In her hands was a butcher knife. She was getting ready to plunge it into whoever was below her.

His pulse pounded. It was Julie.

Howard leapt onto the front steps and tried the front door. It was locked. He stepped back and then lunged forward with his foot, sending the door reeling inwards. The TV had been left on in the living room, filling the house with voices, but he could hear the sounds of struggle from the next room. He ran inside.

Howard stopped short when he got to the dining room. Dan was on the floor with Julie on top of him. From the looks of it, she was about to murder her husband.

Dan was holding his wife's wrist, the blade just inches from his nose. Julie's face was covered in shadow, her eyes sunken into two black recesses below her brows. She moved her head upward at Howard's arrival, but only slightly.

Howard planted his feet on the ground, stabilizing his pistol with both hands. Pain shot through his right arm from the pre-existing wound.

"Don't shoot her, Howard!" Dan screamed.

"Julie—drop the knife now!" he shouted.

The woman shook her hair back and forth, as if trying to block out their voices. With her free hand, she dug at her husband's stomach, tearing at his shirt. Dan screamed in agony, trying to break free.

"Dammit!"

Howard squeezed the trigger. The bullet connected with Julie's right shoulder, sending the knife clattering to the floor. She toppled backwards, her white dress rippling in the air. Dan rolled out from underneath her. He was screaming now — mouthing words that Howard could not hear. The gunshot still rang in Howard's ears, and he was temporarily deaf to the world around him.

Julie was back up again. She threw herself across the room, this time at Howard. Blood dripped from a hole in her shoulder, and her right arm flopped uselessly at her side. Dan reached for her, catching hold of her dress, and she pitched to the side, losing her balance. Her head collided with the corner of the dining room table, and she collapsed to the floor like a sack of laundry.

"Oh my God — no!" Dan screamed.

Howard watched his comrade fall to her side and push away her hair, cupping his hands around her neck — searching for a pulse, but seemingly finding none. The side of her head was sliced open, spilling her life essence onto the wood floor. Dan buried his face in his hands, and then started to stand.

"My daughter!"

"Where is she?" Howard asked.

"In her bedroom...the door is locked." Dan waved toward a key on the floor.

"I'll get her, Dan — just stay with Julie. I'll call for an ambulance."

Howard retrieved the key and headed down the hall toward the closed door on the right, his arms shaking. He'd done his best to prepare for this, but he felt a tinge of emotion. He shouldn't have come here. He should have stayed at home.

He fumbled with the lock for a few seconds, finally finding the keyhole. He pushed the door open with his foot, and then let his pistol lead the way.

A minute later he returned to Dan's side.

"The window's open," he said. "Quinn's gone."

PART TWO
SECRET CHAOS

6

Quinn Madison Lowery had never left home without permission. In fact, there were a lot of things she had never done. As she ran into the night, alone, she wondered if she would ever get the chance to do them.

She liked to think she was a good kid, and respectful to her mom and dad. Besides, her father was a police officer, and he could sniff out what she was up to before she even knew it herself. He was smart like that.

"Don't forget, I was a kid once myself," he often reminded her.

She wasn't perfect, though. Far from it. A year ago, she had been caught shoplifting at the local grocery store.

Quinn loved to read. She had been reading ever since she could remember—books, comics, magazines, or anything else she could get ahold of. For the most part, her parents were supportive of her habit. This time, however, her mom had been in a hurry, and wasn't in the mood to indulge Quinn's literary appetite.

"Not today, honey — I mean it."

All she'd wanted was one of the newest tabloid magazines. Inside, there was an article on one of her favorite actresses. Quinn didn't see the harm in it.

Unable to convince her mother, she'd tucked the magazine up into her shirt, securing the bottom in the waist of her blue jeans. She remembered how it felt — smooth against her stomach, but at the same time bulky and uncomfortable. In order to get out the door with it, she had needed to walk upright, arching her back like there was a metal rod in her spine. She remembered feeling a tinge of excitement as she walked out of the store, and then a moment of fear as she realized she would have to sit down in the car.

"What's wrong with you, Quinn? Why are you doubled over like that?" her mom had asked.

Quinn tried to bend down, but the thick folds of the magazine were digging into her gut, and it hurt too much to move.

"Do you have something in your shirt? Get over here!" her mother had demanded. "Lift it up!"

Quinn had revealed the magazine, her cheeks stiff, and the blood draining from her face. Without a word, her mother had snatched it from her grasp, returning to the store to pay for it. While she was gone, Quinn started to panic. What would they do with her? Would she be sent to jail? Would her father arrest her? It was such a small town—she was sure everyone would find out her secret.

Quinn Madison Lowery was a thief, they would say. The thought made her nauseous.

Her mother had driven home in silence, the look on her face enough to fill a thousand conversations. But that had been the end of it. As far as Quinn knew, her mother had never spoken of the incident to her father.

Quinn promised herself she would never make the same mistake again. After all, she was ten years old now. She had learned a lot since she was nine.

Now, as she climbed from her bedroom window and into the night, she wondered how much trouble she would be in. Would she ever be allowed to leave the house again? Her legs scraped against the windowsill, creating red marks in the pits of her knees, and she swiveled her arms and dropped to the ground below. Her heart pounded in her chest with fear.

She fell on her butt, using her hands as a cushion to break her fall. Inside the house, she could hear grunting and banging, as if a wrestling match were taking place in the dining room. She heard a voice, too, but wasn't sure if it was her father's. She couldn't take any chances. He may have a knife, too.

The air tasted dark and thick, and she struggled to catch her breath.

As she fled into the night, Quinn wondered

who would punish her when she finally returned. In just a few hours, her world had been turned upside down.

7

HOWARD PAUSED ON THE LOWERYS' front porch, searching for movement in all directions. His cruiser sat where he had left it, and the garage door was still closed. To his right, he saw the open window where Quinn must have exited, curtains wafting outwards in the subtle breeze. He couldn't imagine she had gotten far.

"I'll find her, Dan," he called behind him. "Wait here a minute — she can't be far."

Inside the house, the officer moaned, his grief spilling from the dining room and out into the night. The TV blared over him, playing the theme song of a classic detective show. Howard considered turning it off, but descended the steps instead.

He tried to put himself in the little girl's frame of mind. Where would she have run? He looked to his right, past the few trees that lined the property. The closest house was a few yards away. An old woman lived there. He thought her name was Sadie, but he couldn't recall. Either way, she must be approaching her eighties, and was probably fast asleep. Her house was black inside, offering no sign that she had received an unexpected guest.

The Reynolds family lived in the house on the left. Howard knew them well. They would often stop at the Lowery's for an evening barbeque. Their house, too, was dark. A single porch light illuminated the front steps, casting shadows like fingers into the yard. If they had received a knock at the door, he was certain they would have called the police by now.

Howard swept the perimeter of the house. In just a few minutes, he cleared the front and then made his way to the backyard. He almost tripped over a piece of wood on the ground, and realized it was the side of Julie's garden.

Four pieces of plywood flanked the sides, surrounding a variety of green, leafy plants in the center. He strained his eyes, but didn't recognize anything human amongst them. No figure was hiding in the interior.

The rest of the backyard was open, and he didn't see any other places Quinn could hide. He checked the far side of the house, but to no avail. If he had been the little girl, he probably would have run quite a ways before stopping. He imagined her trust was thin at this point. It wasn't every day that your mother came at you with a kitchen knife.

Howard thought back to what he had seen in the house. Julie was barely recognizable—a soulless, corpse-like version of her former self. Her eyes had seemed to penetrate through him, intent on destruction. Howard shuddered and bit his lip, trying to forget what he had seen.

This had to happen, he reminded himself.

He gripped his gun. A sudden glow in the distance drew his attention. Several hundred yards away, on what must have been an adjacent street, a light had just gone on in one of the houses.

Howard contemplated using his radio, and then withdrew his hand. It didn't matter, now, anyways. Nothing did.

He sucked in a breath and sprinted toward the light.

QUINN RAN UNTIL HER CHEEKS were red, her stomach was tight, and her legs began to tire. She fought the urge to look back, fearing that someone would grab her if she did. Surely, whenever the scuffle ended, somebody would come looking for her. Maybe even to kill her. Her heart leapt against her ribcage. She needed to get help — and fast.

She hadn't dared stop at the neighbors. The noise would have attracted immediate attention. Something told her she needed to get farther away in order to have a fighting chance.

Behind Shunpike Lane was another street — she forgot the name, but it was a nice road, and full of houses. Often, she would ride her bike there, watching the families and children. She used to dream about living there someday. The houses seemed nicer in that neighborhood. Now the houses hung in the distance: dark shapes that seemed strange and unfamiliar. She'd never been there at night.

Quinn wondered what time it was. It must

be late—not a single house seemed active. The one closest to her had a small picnic table in the backyard. She could make out a dim glow from one of the back windows, probably from a nightlight. The Anderson family used to live here, but someone new had moved in last month. Her mother had been meaning to stop in to welcome them to the neighborhood. Back when things had still been normal.

There was a sliding glass door in back, but she realized knocking would make her visible to anyone behind her. Instead, she walked past the picnic table and began to cut through to the front yard. As she did so, the rear light flicked on. She stopped suddenly and turned back to face it.

A shadow stood behind the glass, surveying the lot outside. The lights inside the house were off, so Quinn could only make out a silhouette. The person remained still except for their head, which swiveled from side to side. Quinn hugged the side of the yard, hidden from the glow. She wanted to cry out, but her inner voice told her to stay still.

The shadow slid its hands down the glass, as if wiping at some unseen condensation. Its fingers were long and curved, and it rapped at the pane with its fingernails. She wondered if the hands' owner was a man or a woman. The person seemed to move unnaturally—unlike anyone she had ever seen. Without realizing it, she held her breath.

Quinn looked to her left, where another

house sat in silence. If anybody else had been awakened by the light, they hadn't let on. Across the street, she made out another row of houses. They remained still. She looked back to the patio window.

The head and hands had stopped moving. She squinted, and could now make out a pair of ovals where the person's eyes should have been, reflecting in the moonlight. They seemed to be staring in her direction.

Quinn had been spotted.

She ran, letting out bursts of breath as her legs kicked into gear. Behind her, she heard the sound of a sliding glass door being thrust open.

She crossed the side yard and into the front, the dry grass crunching under her feet. Although she wanted to look back, she pushed on. She entered the roadway, heard another pair of feet hit the grass behind her. She pictured the long fingers swaying at the person's side, preparing to wrap around her neck like pieces of rope.

Hurry up, Quinn, she thought. Something wet hit her cheeks, and she realized she was crying. She wished her mother and father could be here, that they could help her. But they were in on the whole thing. Whatever the thing was.

She was on her own.

Pavement gave way to grass again, and she flew up the walkway to the nearest house. She banged on the door and rang the bell at the same time.

"Help!" she cried, but her voice was raspy and weak.

Footsteps slapped on the pavement behind her, drawing ever closer. She didn't have time to wait. *Keep moving,* she thought. Quinn stumbled through the darkness to the side of the house, heading deeper into the property. When she hit the backyard, a voice echoed from the front. She dared to glance behind her.

"Hello? Who's out there?" the person called.

The front lights came on, and she heard the homeowner open the screen door. Her pursuer stopped in the road.

"What do you want?" the homeowner asked.

The figure hovered in the street, arms at its sides. Quinn gripped the edge of the house, wondering if the shadow could still see her. She hoped not.

"I'm going to call the police!" the homeowner threatened. It was a man's voice, and his words rang with fear.

The figure crouched, its arms hanging low to the ground. It hissed into the night, and Quinn pictured a tongue as long as its fingers, sliding across a pair of razor-sharp teeth. She kept quiet, wondering if it could hear the sound of her heartbeat. It certainly seemed loud to her. She drew a breath and held it, wishing as hard as she could that she were invisible.

The figure moved, arms swinging at its sides, heading for the front of the house. The homeowner continued to yell, but the figure ignored his warning.

Quinn moved along the side of the house, toward the front, until she was right at the edge. She could make out the homeowner now—it was Mr. Philips, one of her neighbors. His white hair gleamed in the porch light, and he was leaning out into the night, waving one arm at the intruder. Mr. Philips had helped her fill her bike tire once when she had gotten a flat. He didn't seem quite as friendly now.

"What the hell?" he yelled.

Before he could react, the figure was on him, pulling him out of the house. She heard ripping sounds as it tore at his chest, and then screaming as Mr. Philips fell to the ground. His hands flew up to protect his face, but the figure cast them aside, wrapping its fingers around the man's skull and its thumbs pushing into where his eye sockets would be.

Quinn held back a sob. She wanted to help. But what could she do? She was only ten years old. The thing screeched, and she saw blood splash onto the door. Quinn covered her eyes and cried—for her mother, for Mr. Philips, and for herself, knowing that she would never reach another birthday.

9

HOWARD REACHED THE HOUSE IN minutes, his boots pounding hard on the grass. A single light faced outward in the backyard, revealing a picnic table and an assortment of lawn chairs. The sliding glass door had been left open, as if someone had recently exited or entered.

He held his gun in front of him, watching for any signs of activity.

"Police!" he shouted.

He was met with silence. He advanced a few steps — and then heard a scream pierce the night air. It sounded like it was coming from past the house, across the next street. Howard swiveled and worked his way around front, toward the source of the noise.

His arm brushed his side, and he squirmed in pain. He sprinted past the house and into the road, ignoring the burning in his bicep. Directly ahead of him, illuminated by a porch light, a figure was bent over another man, unwrapping his insides and pulling them onto the walkway.

Howard aimed his gun in front of him,

approaching the assailant and victim. The victim had been mutilated beyond recognition—his face condensed into a soupy puddle of blood and eyeballs. The walkway was stained with flesh and innards, and the figure sifted through the remains with delicate fingers.

The suspect looked up and raised its hands in the air, dangling pieces of detached skin. Its eyes blazed into Howard, devoid of life, eerily reminiscent of the look Julie had given him earlier.

Howard squeezed the trigger, firing a round into the figure's head. It slammed backwards into the door, and he fired twice more into its chest. The emotion he'd felt before was fading.

He was already starting to feel the way he had felt with Frank.

Things were going exactly as planned.

Several lights appeared around him, and Howard tensed up. Heads peered through windows and doors cracked cautiously open. In the distance, behind the house, he heard the sound of a little girl screaming. The noise faded into the distance, her cries softening with each step.

In an instant, he knew it was Quinn. And he knew exactly where she was headed.

Quinn was on the move again. This time, she wasn't going to stop. She had a destination in mind. She wasn't sure why she hadn't thought of it before, but she was sure glad she thought of it now.

She wasn't ready to die. Not yet.

She kept running, dragging her feet like dumbbells. She screamed when gunshots rang out behind her, but continued on. A few sparse trees swayed in the wind, pointing her onwards, leading her from one street to the next. Only a few more neighborhoods to go, and she would be there.

Her throat started to burn. The doctor said she had mild asthma—not the kind that you needed to use an inhaler for, but enough that she should take it easy. In gym class, she was often excused from the more rigorous activities. She felt herself gasping for air now, but she did not slow down.

Ahead, she saw a familiar house on the horizon. She only needed to cross one more street to get there. Her feet hit pavement once again, and she prayed that she had outrun whoever might be following her.

Up ahead, Sheriff Turner's patrol car sat in the driveway. She wiped the tears from her eyes and felt a sense of relief wash over her. The house was dark, but he must be home. He had to be. She ran up the front steps and mashed her hands against the doorbell, hearing it ring inside the house. After a few seconds, she heard footsteps plodding through the house.

Thank God, she thought.

Quinn doubled over, her pulse beating through

the side of her neck, and tried to breathe deeply. She needed to calm down so she could explain what had happened. She looked back, but saw no signs of her pursuer. The door creaked open behind her, and the familiar figure of Sheriff Turner filled the doorway.

"Sheriff," she tried to speak, but no sound came out.

She ran inside the house, under his outstretched arm, and motioned for him to shut the door. The lights were off, and she edged towards the couch, looking over her shoulder to make sure no one was following her inside. Though it was dark, rays of moonlight filtered through the windows and into the living room. Her foot struck something on the floor, and she paused suddenly and looked down.

Mrs. Turner's body lay in the center of the rug, curled up in a ball. An awful odor rose from the body. She looked dead.

"W-What happened?" Quinn whispered, turning.

Sheriff Turner stood in the doorway like a statue, his arm still propped against the frame. It appeared he hadn't moved since letting her inside. At the sound of her voice, his body came to life, and he let the screen door slam shut. He lifted an enormous leg and moved towards her.

"Sheriff—it's me, Quinn Lowery," she said, backing up against the couch.

The man wheezed, placing one calf in front of the other, shaking the living room with each footstep. Beads of sweat glistened from his forehead and rolled down his face. She backed up farther, hitting the couch and falling to a sitting position.

She began to cry.

The sheriff made a grab for her leg, and she swung it upwards and out of reach, letting out a stifled scream. She threw her arms over the couch and pulled herself to the other side. Something sharp on the fabric ripped at her leg, and she cried out. She slid over the couch and onto the floor, just as Sheriff Turner landed on the cushions in front. His weight slid the couch backwards and into her shins, and she screamed in pain.

She limped towards the kitchen. A large lamp hugged the wall at the entrance, and she threw it down behind her to create a barricade. The Sheriff grunted as he regained his footing. Quinn forged ahead, avoiding the kitchen table and heading for the back door. She reached it and fumbled for the handle.

The doorknob turned, and then stopped. The door was locked. Her hands slid wildly around the knob, and she finally found the button on the center, twisting it sideways and releasing the catch.

The door wouldn't budge. It must be dead-bolted.

Sheriff Turner was in the kitchen now, making his way toward her, and she began to panic. Her eyes were starting to adjust, and she searched for anything she could use as a weapon. The counters contained a mess of appliances—a toaster, a blender, and some dirty dishes—but nothing of use. It was too late. He was upon her now, and he flung his arm forward, reaching for her head.

Quinn tried to duck, but not in time. She felt a piece of hair rip from her scalp, and her eyes stung with pain. She scooted on the floor, the vinyl cold on her fingertips and knees, and slid her way across the kitchen and back into the living room.

There was a door on her right, and she yanked it open and slammed it shut behind her, wedging herself between a mop and bucket. She held the inside handle, waiting for it to turn in her fingers, and choked back a sob.

On the other side of the door, she heard the Sheriff knocking over the kitchen table and chairs, destroying his own belongings to get to her. She imagined what would happen when he found her hiding in the closet, weaponless and alone. Her eyes welled up, and she began to shake.

10

HOWARD RACED TOWARD SULLIVAN AVENUE. If he'd calculated correctly, the road was about four blocks away — cutting through backyards, of course. He could have returned to his cruiser, but he would have lost precious time.

I should probably return home, he thought.

But something pressed him onward. Whether it was the adrenaline or the taste of the night air, Howard felt more alive than he had in years.

And that feeling was keeping him going.

He perked up his ears, listening for signs of the girl. He hadn't heard any screaming now for a few minutes. Either the girl had wised up, or she had already reached her destination. The thought struck him that she may have fallen prey to another attacker.

As he ran, Howard wondered if he had guessed correctly as to her whereabouts. If she had taken another turn somewhere in the dark, it would be almost impossible to find her. He would need to use the spotlights on his cruiser.

As he passed through the next street, he saw

lights flicking on from the houses around him. Presumably the homeowners had heard the commotion. In several doorways, shadows stared at him, and he felt an even deeper sense of unease.

The grass crunched underfoot, fried from the desert heat and lack of water. He imagined that if he stopped to inspect it, he would see Quinn's footprints leading the way. The radio crackled in his ear, breaking his concentration.

"*Howard, you there*?" Mickey said.

Howard reached up to his shoulder and silenced the radio.

As he finally reached the fourth street, he noticed all the lights were off. There was no sign of activity among the residents. Perhaps Quinn had veered off in another direction, or she had stopped screaming just shy of Sullivan Avenue, leaving its residents blissfully asleep. He glanced farther up the road, and squinted into the night. His initial observation had been incorrect. One set of porch lights *was* on, near the end of the road. Now that he had noticed them, they seemed to illuminate the house in the night like a beacon.

Sheriff Turner's patrol car sat in the driveway.

Either his boss was getting ready to leave the house—already made aware of the night's events—or else a little girl had knocked on his door just short of midnight. Howard crossed the road, running now.

He drew close to the car, holding his gun in front of him. The screen was shut, but the storm door had been left open. As he started up the walkway, he heard a tremendous crash from inside.

"Sheriff?" he called in.

The banging continued. A girl's shriek rang out from within. Howard threw open the door, leading with his pistol, and entered the living room. A massive shadow hugged the back of the room. It was ramming against a door on the other side.

"Police! Hold it right there!" Howard yelled.

He felt for the light switch. Thankfully, his memory served him well, and the room lit up. He had been to the Sheriff's house plenty of times, but never on police business. His jaw dropped as he surveyed the scene.

The first thing he saw was the body of Mrs. Laney Turner. The woman was facedown in the middle of the room, her head caved in. The busted frames of her glasses lay beside her, stuck to the wood floor in a collage of blood. Clumps of her hair covered the carpet.

Sheriff Turner stood behind the couch, his hands raised above his head. Black streaks covered his eyes, as if they had been injected with vials of India ink. He had ripped open the hall closet, tearing the frail wooden door from its hinges, and it lay sideways by his feet. His massive figure concealed the majority of the doorframe, but Howard could see through his legs.

Quinn Lowery sat amongst the cleaning

products, arms tucked over her head. She whimpered as she saw him, as if he, too, had come to attack her.

The sheriff grunted, turning his attention to the new visitor. He moved towards the front door.

Howard gritted his teeth and fired the pistol. He continued to squeeze the trigger, firing one round after the next, until he had emptied the entire clip into his boss. The bullets riddled the fat man's body, pulling corks of flesh from his stomach and spilling red fluid beneath. The sheriff's eyes rolled in his head, and he collapsed with a *thud* onto the floor.

The girl began to bawl. She put her head between her legs, hair billowing over her knees. Howard looked at her and then at the body on the floor. The sheriff lay in a pool of blood, his dead wife just ten feet away. Howard felt nothing.

Nothing at all.

He lowered his gun. For the first time that night, a sense of calm swept over him.

"Come with me," he said to the girl. Although he didn't realize it, his lips had curved upwards into a smile.

Howard and Quinn walked in silence. The girl trailed behind, sniffling quietly to herself, but didn't utter a word.

After taking care of the sheriff, Howard had

warned Quinn to keep her composure and remain quiet. He instructed her to stick to his side as they made their way back to the Lowery residence. He'd been harsh, but it was what she needed to hear. The gunshots had attracted enough attention.

Even still, the streets seemed eerily silent. Many of the houses still had their lights blazing, but Howard no longer saw any shadows in the doorways. It was as if the residents had returned to bed, unaware of the danger. *Or else they were roaming the streets, looking for victims*, he thought.

Howard stopped suddenly. A sound had emitted from a pair of trees in front of them. The girl stopped behind him.

He aimed his gun. An object moved behind one of the tree trunks. He saw a flash of white from near the ground, and then something jutting out into the open. A tail. Howard lowered his weapon. A cat slinked towards them, purring. He imagined they had caught the animal mid-chase — probably on the hunt for a mouse or some other rodent. It rubbed against the girl's legs, and he waved his arms at it, sending it scurrying back behind the trees.

Howard glanced around them in all directions, but no other figures emerged. He took the opportunity to withdraw a cellphone from his pocket. A text message was waiting for him.

Status? It read.

He returned his gun to its holster, and signaled for the girl to wait. Her eyes fell downwards, and she stared at her shoes in compliance. Using his thumbs, he drafted a reply.

On schedule.

He hit the 'send' button, and returned the phone to his pocket. Later, he would break it into pieces and discard the remnants in various locations. Just to be sure. Though he doubted anyone would ever make the connection. The cellphone had been sent to him by mail, probably purchased from a remote location. He knew he could trust the phone's sender.

Right now, he needed to focus to ensure his survival. That was what was expected of him. To monitor the townspeople, to ensure all went as planned. Only when the destruction of St. Matthews was complete would he be able to relax. He withdrew his pistol once again and began to move. The girl fell in line behind him.

Out of respect for Dan, he had decided to return the little girl—but that was it. Afterwards, the pair would be on their own, along with the rest of this God-forsaken town.

PART THREE
BROKEN FOUNDATION

11

DAN CLUNG TO HIS DEAD wife for what seemed like an eternity. He parted her hair, kissed her forehead, and tried to ignore the fact that she looked nothing like the woman he loved. The gash on her head had stopped bleeding, but a puddle of blood on the floor served as evidence that she had once been alive.

His mind was spinning, still trying to comprehend what had happened. For a second, he felt like he was out of his own body, looking down at himself.

He needed to find his daughter. Where the hell was Howard? And where the hell were the medics? Howard had called them, hadn't he?

His eyes darted around the room, passing over the wreckage that had once been his dining room. Julie's chair lay on its back. Several of the rungs had cracked, and the back had started to separate from the frame. Next to it was the knife, which gave off only a dull shine — far less threatening without a hand to wield it.

He had dropped his pistol on the floor next

to him, freeing up both hands to cradle his wife's body. The gun seemed to beckon to him now, a subtle reminder of his duties as a police officer and father. He felt a breeze pass through the house, kicking up a lock of Julie's hair and draping it across his face. Howard must have left the door open.

Dan began to think about getting up, about releasing his death-grip on a woman who had already embraced death. They'd been married for eleven years. He had known her since high school. He remembered how beautiful she had looked at their wedding—how brave she had been during the birth of their child. He gritted his teeth and fought back the tears. He needed to let go. He needed to move. His daughter needed him.

He let his hands slip from her body, wiped his arm across his face to dry his eyes, and gently eased his wife back to the floor. Quinn was still out there, and if he lost her too, he would have lost everything.

Before he could stand, a pair of footsteps clapped against the pavement outside. *The rest of the force*, he thought. He was sure that Mickey and Sheriff Turner would be on their way—in fact he was surprised they hadn't made it already. As the noises continued, he realized something sounded off. His fellow officers would have announced their presence. The footsteps he heard seemed muffled, as if the owners were trying to conceal their arrival.

Dan's police instincts kicked in, and he scurried to the far end of the dining room, positioning himself between the table and the living room doorway.

The screen door at the front of the house banged against the frame. He considered calling out, but decided against it. He aimed the pistol in front of him, propping his arms on one of the chairs.

The TV volume seemed to increase, and he strained to hear over it. Something scraped against the wall in the living room, and Dan's body went rigid.

Someone was in the next room.

A hand entered the doorway, pawing at the air in front of it, testing the waters. After the appendage came a torso, and then a full body, black eyes scanning back and forth as it wormed sideways into the dining room. Dan recoiled at the figure, whose face was twisted and wild. It idled towards him, feeling its way forward, heading right for the table.

Dan fired a round, shattering its knee and sending it reeling to the floor. Another was behind it, this one faster than the last, already veering around Julie's body and gaining ground. He fired again, splintering the side off of the chair opposite him, missing his target. The chair toppled backwards, landing on Julie's body.

Dan was on his feet now, scooting around the table. The first attacker fumbled on its broken knee, contending with the chair, and its companion pushed past it without skipping a beat. The creatures—*things*—spewed bile from their mouths, salivating onto the floor below as they tried to reach him.

He reached the living room doorway. Behind him, he heard the remaining furniture topple over. He crossed the room, panting, and stopped at the front screen door. Outside, three more were headed up the walkway. They groaned when they saw him.

"Oh, fuck," he whispered.

Dan slammed the front door shut, dead bolting it. He whipped around, gun in front of him, and felt something grab his arm. One of the first houseguests had caught up to him. Its fingers were cold on his skin, wrapping around his wrist like icicles.

He kicked forward, connecting with its stomach, and sent it toppling backwards into the couch. He raised his pistol and fired into it, gritting his teeth. Three bullets passed through its chest, blood and bile rippling out from the wounds. The creature sunk down onto the couch cushions, and then stood up again, unfazed.

He heard the sound of nails on the front screen, and then something pounding on the front door. If he didn't get out of this house, Dan was certain it would become his tomb.

He skirted around the couch, avoiding the outstretched hands of the creature in the living room, and entered the dining room again. The first creature was still on the floor, crawling on its knees, coming towards him. He shot off a round into its head and watched it collapse to the floor.

He swiveled again, facing the remaining creature from the living room—this time aiming for its forehead. Maybe that was the key. *Just like the goddamn movies*, he thought, realizing at once how insane that sounded. His heart sunk when he pulled the trigger.

He was out of bullets.

12

"I don't want to go back home," Quinn whispered.

Howard looked at her, but his eyes seemed distant. He was holding his gun in one hand and a cellphone in the other. He kept checking the phone, as if expecting someone to call. His arms were crooked upwards, and his muscles bulged underneath his shirt.

Quinn had always looked up to him. Whenever he visited, he was especially nice. On her last birthday, he had even brought her a stack of books to read—introducing her to some of the classics that he had enjoyed as a child. Now, everything seemed different. *Howard* seemed different.

"We have to go back," he said. "Your father is there."

But her mother was too. A pang of fear went through her stomach as she pictured her mother shoving her into the bedroom, knife in hand.

"Are my mom and dad okay?"

Howard looked at the phone again, typing on the keypad.

"Sure, Quinn. They're both fine. I'm going to take you home to them."

He kept his eyes on the cellphone, but she saw him watching her out of the corner of his eye. He wasn't telling the truth. She could sense it. But why would he lie? What would he say when they got to her house and the truth was right there in front of them?

She pictured Sheriff Turner's body in the living room, bloated and bleeding. She didn't know much about gunshot wounds, but Howard hadn't even checked for a pulse — he'd just left the man on the floor. It was as if he wasn't even concerned about him. Or maybe he knew something she didn't. She watched him type away on the cellphone. Who was he talking to? And why were they standing here?

Howard finished his message. A few seconds later, the phone vibrated.

Quinn moved closer to the officer. In the dark, she could almost make out the incoming text message. She forced herself to cry again, inching towards him.

"It's okay," he said, but he made no physical effort to console her.

She was standing next to him now; her eyes were level with the phone. The screen glowed yellow. She shuddered when she read the words.

Every last one must go.

Quinn ran.

13

DAN WAVED THE EMPTY PISTOL in front of him, but the creature kept coming. It sidestepped Julie's body and then walked over the body of its dead companion. Its eyes rolled back into its head, and it groaned.

He stepped backwards into the kitchen, still holding the gun, wishing he had the time or the means to reload. His palms were sweaty, and he struggled to keep his balance. He bumped into the roll of paper towels, and it skittered backwards, unraveling to the end of the tube.

The creature advanced.

Dan spotted his keys — they were on the counter to his left. A few steps further, and he could make a grab for them.

"Stay back!" he shouted.

The thing's mouth opened, revealing a row of bloodied teeth. If it understood him, the words had little effect. Dan threw his arm sideways, succeeding only in pushing the keys farther down the counter. He made another grab. This time, he closed his fist around them.

He eyed the knife holder. In his haste, he'd already passed by it. He could lunge toward it, but that would put him in harm's way. The creature stood beside it, mouth hanging open. He needed to get out of the house.

He reached behind him, found the door handle, and stepped back into the garage. He slammed the door closed, then used his keys to lock it. The creature smashed against the other side, but the door held. For now.

Dan's cruiser was where he had left it, and the garage door remained closed. He ran to the car door, fumbling with the keychain. He saw his house key, his locker key, and a slew of others. Where the hell was the car key? *Focus*, his mind screamed.

The creature pounded on the kitchen door, shaking it in the frame. Dan located the key and slipped it into the lock. The car was open now. He flung open the door and hopped inside, and then promptly shut it behind him.

Bam! The kitchen door caved in, whipping against the wall and off the hinges. The creature was loose in the garage now, heading towards the car.

Dan cried out in surprise, turning the key in the ignition.

The car fired up, and he revved the engine. He reached up and hit the garage door opener, watching it open behind him in the rearview mirror. The creature was at the driver's side window, just inches away. Its breath fogged up the glass, and it pounded on the window.

"C'mon, hurry up!" Dan screamed at the garage door.

He threw the car in reverse and hit the gas. The car inched backwards. Dan looked behind him and then rammed on the brakes.

Howard's police cruiser was parked in the driveway, directly behind the garage door. There was no way to get the cruiser out of the garage. Julie's Subaru Outback sat to his right.

The creature hissed at him through the window, its nails scratching on the glass. Dan glanced in his rearview again. The three other things from the front yard had stepped into the garage, and were heading for the cruiser. He looked down at the ignition. The key to the Outback dangled from the chain.

He needed to get to the other car. And fast.

Dan ripped the keys from the ignition and climbed into the passenger seat, knocking over a coffee cup on his way. His gun was on the seat, but it was useless without bullets. He tucked it into his holster anyway, then reached for the door handle. He paused to look around him.

The creature to his left had begun moving around the front of the cruiser. Three others approached the passenger side. The Outback was just a few feet away. If he didn't get out of the cruiser soon, he would be trapped. Dan opened the door and leapt out.

He grabbed hold of the car key and threw it into the Outback, but it was too late. One of the creatures ripped at his shirt collar, tearing him away from the vehicle.

"No!" he shouted.

Dan threw his elbow back and felt it connect with a face. The attacker fell backwards, knocking into its companions, but the three barricaded any escape from the garage.

He was surrounded.

Dan dropped to the floor and pulled himself underneath the Outback. As he did, he heard something clatter onto the floor behind him. *Damn*, he thought. *My keys*. From underneath the car, he saw a parade of shoes stepping around them. His pulse beat through his body, sending a rush of blood to his temples.

Dan wiggled his feet, suddenly feeling claustrophobic. He reached his arm out slowly, but the keys were too far away. He inched towards them, balling his feet and pushing off the garage floor. He could almost reach them. He strained his fingers, watching them leave the protection of the vehicle and enter the open garage. He had almost made it when a cold, fleshy hand grabbed his wrist.

One of the creatures was on the ground, looking back at him with dark eyes. It hissed and pulled on his arm.

"Get the hell off of me!"

He wrenched his hand back, wincing as the

creature's nails scratched his wrist. The other things dropped to their knees and reached underneath the car, inspired by their companion. Dan pulled himself towards the other side, avoiding four sets of hands that were now clawing to get to him.

He glanced towards the passenger side of the vehicle. The garage wall was empty, providing a few feet in which he could maneuver. There were no sets of feet on that side. For now, the coast was clear. He edged himself sideways, and stood up quickly on the opposite side.

One of the creatures roamed towards the trunk, blocking a quick exit out the front of the garage. He looked around, searching for another option. On the back wall, he spotted the gardening tools hanging neatly from their pegs. Amongst them was a pitchfork.

Dan made a dash for it. The creatures had given up on the car and were headed his way. He grabbed the pitchfork from the wall and swung it in front of him.

"C'mon you bastards!"

One of the creatures made a grab for him, and he propelled the tines deep into its stomach, sending it reeling backwards. He pulled back on the handle, watching a rainfall of blood soak its shirt. It staggered, momentarily off balance. He turned the pitchfork sideways and swung it like a baseball bat, propelling the creature into the side of the Outback.

He squeezed past it and towards the back of

the garage. The others were by the trunk, and he gored the first in the neck. It toppled backward, but Dan persisted, plunging the weapon into the mass of flesh behind it, striking each in turn. The creatures tumbled backwards, hitting the floor, and he stood over each of their bodies, ramming the garden tool into one after the other until all movement had stopped.

When he finished, Dan realized he was screaming. He looked down at the creatures, whose bodies were now covered in gaping holes, fluid spilling from their insides. In all his years on the force, he had never killed anyone. In fact, he often prayed that he would retire before getting the chance. He had seen plenty of dead bodies, but none that had met their demise at his own hands.

Dan turned his head and vomited on the garage floor, letting the pitchfork clatter to the ground. When he was finished retching, he dragged the bodies from behind the car, clearing a path to the outside.

He retrieved the keys and started the Outback. He threw it into reverse, and sped down the driveway and out into the road.

Somewhere, his daughter was in danger. He just prayed to God he wasn't too late to save her.

14

THE LITTLE GIRL TOOK OFF running, and Howard chased after her. His attention had been on the cellphone, so she'd taken him by surprise. It didn't matter. She wouldn't get far. The phone vibrated again in his hand, but this time he slid it into his pocket.

They'd been standing next to the side of a house when she took off. A few trees lined the perimeter, and she had slipped through them to the neighboring property. He clutched his gun, unsure of what he might run into. The plan had been set in motion, and soon the streets would start to fill with the infected. *The contamination has begun.*

Ahead of him, Howard saw a small shadow slip around to the front of the house next door. Although he only caught a quick glance, he was pretty sure it was Quinn. He thought for a second about abandoning the chase, about letting fate take its course. Sooner or later, she would run into one of them, and that would be the end of it. Saving her now would only delay the inevitable.

Five years ago, when he had moved to St Matthews, Howard had tried to keep to himself. There was no use in befriending any of his co-workers or socializing with the townspeople—not with what he knew was coming. He tried to focus instead on his training, on honing his physical and mental abilities. After a few years, he had let his guard down.

He had started engaging in the occasional barbeque, a monthly game of pool. The town's fate was sealed, he thought, so he may as well make the most of his time there. The Agent leaders had said to blend in to the community—to act as natural as possible.

Howard felt a tinge of pity for Dan and his family. He had grown closer to them than he had intended. But nobody would escape the contamination. He needed to remind himself of that fact. Helping them now would do nothing.

He would be the only survivor in St. Matthews.

Still, he did intend to find the girl and bring her back to her father—it was the honorable thing to do. And Howard liked to think he was an honorable man. He'd give them a fighting chance.

He rounded the corner of the house and stopped short. Two shadows hugged the siding. The smaller figure lay in the grass, shielding her face and whimpering. It was Quinn, and she was cornered.

The larger shadow turned to face Howard. Its face was a blackened mess, and it snarled at him.

Howard drew back his arm and punched the thing in the head, sending it to the ground. It squirmed, trying to regain its footing, and he aimed his gun between its eyes.

Howard pulled the trigger, and Quinn screamed. The creature went still.

"Let's go, Quinn! If you run again, I'll leave you out here. You understand?"

The girl nodded.

"Get up," he said, softening his tone. "I know this is difficult, but this whole thing is something that needed to happen. The world needs this."

She averted her eyes and followed behind him. He didn't expect her to understand. How could she? She was just a child. He would be glad when all of this was over and done with.

He reached for his phone and read the message that had come in earlier.

Head back to the station and await further instruction.

Howard signaled for the girl to stop as they approached the front of the Lowery residence. The garage door was open now, and the lights from inside spilled out over the driveway and illuminated the yard. The interior was covered in blood, and he saw what looked like the bodies of several infected. Howard's patrol car was still in the driveway, directly behind Dan's. Julie's car was gone.

He looked at the little girl, watching her eyes fill with hope.

"Stay quiet," he said.

Howard crept across the yard and looked through the front windows. The dining room was a mess of broken furniture. The table had been turned on its side, and the chairs were toppled over. Julie's body lay underneath the wreckage. One of the dead things was next to her. He glanced behind him, but Quinn was standing in the middle of the lawn where he had left her. He held up his hand so she would stay put.

The living room was equally destroyed—the TV had been knocked over, and the couch was halfway across the room. However, the place appeared empty. Dan had put up a fight. Howard wasn't surprised, given the officer's track record on the force. Maybe that was why he hadn't turned into one of them yet. Perhaps his body was keeping the infection at bay.

He looked back at Quinn again. She, too, seemed to be holding her own. But it was only a matter of time. He motioned toward his cruiser in the driveway.

"Let's go."

A pair of high beams suddenly lit up the driveway, and Howard shielded his eyes. A car was coming toward them down the road. He wondered if it was Dan.

As the vehicle approached, he could make out two shadows in the front seat, and the outline of police sirens on the roof. There was only one other patrol car unaccounted for. Mickey's. He cursed under his breath, wishing things didn't have to be so complicated.

The cruiser barreled up the driveway and onto the lawn, and then stopped. The windows were down, and he could hear the young officer shouting from inside the vehicle.

"What the fuck? Get off of me, man!"

The passenger was one of the infected, and it clung to Mickey's arm, tearing into the side of his neck with its teeth. The officer cried out in pain, struggling to break free, but unable to undo his seatbelt.

"Help!" he screamed.

The words echoed into the night, bouncing into the garage and past the mound of dead bodies inside. Howard stood motionless, watching his fellow officer flail uselessly at the creature.

"Do something!" Quinn cried out from behind him.

Howard walked to the driver's side of the vehicle and raised the gun. The creature paused mid-bite, its teeth covered in fleshy residue. He squeezed the trigger, firing a round into its head. The thing collapsed into Mickey's neck, falling into the wound it had created.

"Fuck, man," Mickey whispered, blood gurgling through the side of his opened neck.

His eyes were wide, and his arms convulsed at his sides. He reached out for Howard. "Help me, please…"

Howard turned away and walked towards his cruiser.

"In the car," he barked at the girl.

"Where are we going?"

"Back to the station."

"Is my dad there?" Her lips trembled.

Howard looked at her, but didn't answer. His eyes were devoid of emotion.

15

DAN SCOURED THE STREETS OF St. Matthews, searching for any sign of his missing daughter. From Shunpike Lane, he looped around to Treetop Place, and then to Archibald Avenue. He gripped the steering wheel, hands shaking. He tried to dispel the image of his dead wife on the dining room floor.

Julie was gone.

He felt the salty sting of tears hit his lips, and he wiped his face with his sleeve. But Quinn was still alive. She had to be. He pictured his daughter, out on the streets, perhaps fighting for her life just as he had been moments ago. Where could she have gone?

He wracked his brain, trying to determine Quinn's thought process. She was a smart kid — probably smarter than most her age. He held out hope that she had been able to find assistance.

But what if the entire town was infected? What help would there be then? And why hadn't he been stricken with the disease — whatever it was? He looked down at his hands, and then glanced at himself in the rearview mirror. Maybe he was moments away from turning into one of the things himself.

Dan shivered and forced the thought from his mind. Whatever the reason, he was still conscious, still *himself*. At least, he thought he was. And as far as he knew, so were Quinn and Howard.

Dan patted his pocket. His cellphone was still there. *Thank God.* He pulled it out and dialed his senior officer's number. The call went straight to voicemail.

"C'mon, man!"

He dialed again, but with no luck. He scanned his phone for any messages or voicemails, but none had been received. He tucked the device back in his pocket and then looked back at the road. About a hundred feet ahead, just beyond his headlights, he saw a glimmer of movement.

"What the hell?"

A few shadows darted from left to right, and he wiped his eyes to ensure his vision wasn't distorted. A yellow sign passed on his right.

Pedestrian Crossing.

25 MPH.

Dan flicked on his high beams, and then held his breath. A swarm of creatures was in the road, arms hanging at their sides, marching toward a figure lying on the curb. A few were on their knees, ripping into it. *Pulling out the person's insides,* he thought. He hit the brakes, coming to a stop just fifty feet away. Their heads seemed to turn in unison.

There had to be about twenty of the things.

Dan threw the car into reverse. The creatures ran at him, hissing and spitting in an attempt to get to the Outback. He revved the engine, and the car rolled backwards, but not fast enough. One of the creatures tore at the driver's side mirror, ripping it clean off the vehicle. Another flailed its arms at the hood. Others flanked the passenger's side, banging on the windows.

Dan shouted at them, swerving the wheel in an attempt to throw them off. He felt the tires run over a pair of feet, and saw one of the things fall. He stomped the brake, bringing the car to a halt, and then threw it into drive. The things pounded harder on the windows. He hit the gas and sped forward.

He aimed the car straight ahead, where a few stragglers had begun to congregate. They raised their arms and moved towards the vehicle.

"That's right, keep coming!"

Dan plowed into three of the things, hurling them over the hood of the Outback and back onto the pavement. The others had fallen behind, unable to catch the speeding vehicle.

Suddenly he was free, driving into the night, the chaos behind him. Even with the windows up, he could still smell the pungent odor of blood and decay finding its way through the vents. He rolled down the window, but only to a crack. *What has this world come to?*

His cellphone rang, and his heart skipped a beat. He answered the call.

"Hello?"

A voice whispered from the other end.

"He's got Quinn."

Dan looked down at the phone. It was Mickey.

"Who has her? Mickey, are you ok?"

"H-Howard has her. They're headed to the station."

Mickey's voice sounded labored, as if he was speaking underwater. Dan felt a wave of nausea creep over him.

"Where are you?" Dan asked.

His friend paused.

"Don't t-trust him, Dan."

The call disconnected.

16

THE LITTLE GIRL SQUIRMED IN the backseat of the cruiser. Howard had put her there to ensure she wouldn't try running again. He would bring her to the station, and then he would contact her father. Fate should take its course from there. He hoped they didn't meet up again—for their sake.

So far, the streets were empty. Either the infection was still spreading, or the residents were elsewhere, searching for victims. Howard felt a tickle in his throat, and coughed into his hand. He looked down, expecting for a brief moment to see blood on his hand. *Just like his mother had seen years ago, when she had been diagnosed with cancer.* But he knew better. He'd been careful.

Instead of abusing his body the way so many others did, he'd dedicated his life to physical perfection. The Agent leaders had shown him a better way. Humanity was overdue for a cleansing, and only the strongest would survive.

He reached between the seats and retrieved a bottle of water that he had stored there. He twisted off the cap and drank from it. At home, he had several storerooms full of food and drink—enough to last him a year or so, he figured. Plenty of time to outlast the infection.

The Agent leaders had warned him before the contamination was to begin. He'd been prepared. A few weeks prior, he'd received the text message. It was one he'd been waiting on for five years.

It has begun.

Since then, he'd been watching, waiting for the first signs.

Each year, around this time, he received a package in the mail containing a new cellphone. He would carefully discard the old one and destroy the envelope it had come in. Updates had been few and far between, but he'd been kept informed.

Now, he was using the phone to report the progress in St. Matthews. Due to the town's small size and remote location, Howard guessed it was one of the first to be infected. *A trial run for what was to come.*

The information Howard had was limited. He'd been told that the virus would start with the food and water supply, and that he should avoid anything produced after a certain date. But he also knew that the Agents had infiltrated numerous sectors of society—there were plenty of other ways to spread the disease. According to the leaders, he would be briefed as necessary. His survival had been guaranteed. When he was certain everything was progressing as planned, he would retreat back to his house—to wait until the infection had run its course.

The world needed a change. Humanity had abused the earth, destroying their bodies and the environment, succumbing to selfishness and materialism. He had seen everything clearly when his mother died. He had changed his own ways. He had given up his vices.

It was too bad others couldn't see the same thing—that they couldn't realize the flaws in their existence. Now they would suffer the ultimate consequence.

He felt honored to be a part of the first phase. Someday, he might be remembered for being one of the pioneers of the new world.

"Howard?" the girl called out from the backseat.

He sat upright, replacing the water bottle.

"What do you want?"

"Can I get out now? You can drop me off here. I'll be fine."

"I can't do that," he said. "I have to take you back to your father, at the station."

The girl hugged her arms across her chest.

"Does he even know I'm here?"

"Yes," Howard lied.

He could tell she didn't believe him. But it didn't matter. Not anymore.

They were just a few blocks from the station. Howard noticed a few shadows at the side of the road. The cruiser's headlights revealed two creatures picking away at a carcass. They looked up at the passing vehicle and took a few steps toward it as he drove by.

"Not tonight," he muttered.

A few seconds later, Howard pulled into the station. The parking lot was empty. He parked the cruiser and opened the back door, motioning for the girl to get out. She slid out of the backseat and onto the pavement, her eyes darting around the lot. He grabbed her arm and led her to the front door of the station.

The building appeared intact. He unlocked the door, pulled the girl inside, and then locked it behind them.

"This way," he said.

He led her down the corridor toward the jail cell. For a second, he envisioned Frank's body inside, still covered in the blue blanket. The cell had since been cleaned, but he could make out a small red stain underneath the bench, and he grimaced. He unlocked the door and pulled it open, its hinges groaning in protest.

"Inside."

The girl looked at him and began to cry.

"I don't want to go in there, Howard."

She looked up at him, her face streaked with tears. He relaxed his grip on her arm, and then felt her slip through his fingers. She ran for the door.

Howard lunged after her, catching hold of her shirt and pulling her backwards. She flailed in his arms, screaming. He threw her into the cell, locked the door, and headed for the corridor.

Then he took out his cellphone.

17

Dan turned off his lights as he pulled into the police station. He was still reeling from what he had heard. Mickey's voice played over and over in his head.

"Don't trust him, Dan."

He had tried calling the officer back several times, but the call had gone to voicemail. What had Mickey meant? In the midst of what was going on, the cryptic warning sent a shiver of fear through Dan's body. Howard had been his closest friend on the force for five years. What ill intent could he possibly have?

At the same time, he also felt a sense of relief. From the sounds of it, his daughter was alive. He just needed to get to her as soon as possible.

A single cruiser sat in the police station lot. Dan eyed the license plate, confirming that it was Howard's. He parked his car and shut off the engine. The lights were on in the station, but the painted glass windows blocked his view of the inside. As he stepped outside the vehicle, he remembered there were cameras in the parking lot. He hoped Howard wasn't watching them.

He felt for his gun, which was still in its holster. Without bullets, it would be next to useless in the event of an attack. He needed more ammunition.

Dan drew the weapon anyway and crept across the open parking lot. He stopped briefly at Howard's cruiser, peering inside. A few bottles of water and some wrappers lay on the passenger seat. To his surprise, the doors were unlocked, as if Howard had been in a hurry. He opened the door and looked inside. Between the seats was a police baton. *Better than nothing*, he thought to himself. He gently closed the door.

He crossed the rest of the lot to the front door and tugged at the handle. It was locked. He inserted his key and opened the station. Once inside, he scanned the parking lot for the creatures, and then locked the door behind him.

The front corridor was empty. To his left was the door to the locker room. To his right, he saw the door to the main office. There were two other doors — one to the supply room and one to the janitor's closet. The entrance to the jail cell was at the opposite end. He heard voices. One of them grew louder as he approached.

"Howard, please let me out!"

It was Quinn. Had Howard locked her in the jail cell?

Dan began to shake. He felt the urge to dart down the hall, throw open the door at the end, and help her. But he needed to be cautious. Their lives depended on it.

His mind raced. How could Howard have turned on him? The man had stood by his side for years, had always proved himself to be a trustworthy ally. Hell, he'd even eaten meals with Dan's family, had given his daughter gifts for her birthday. Was he infected like the rest of them? Why else would he do this?

The thought made him sick.

Dan heard movement from behind the door up ahead. It sounded like someone was getting ready to exit. He hugged the left side of the corridor, and then ducked into the locker room, gripping the baton to his chest.

He heard the door creak open in the corridor, and then footsteps echoing off the walls.

"Howard, please! Don't leave me in here!" Quinn yelled.

The door slammed shut. Dan held his breath, listening to the man approach. Howard couldn't be more than ten feet away, on the other side of the locker room wall. Dan pressed his cheek against a row of lockers, the metal cold against his cheek.

The footsteps ceased. The echoes tapered off, and the station fell silent.

Had he been spotted on the cameras? Was Howard aware that he was in the station—maybe even aware of his location in the locker room?

Inside the lockers, just inches away, were spare weapons, as well as ammunition. He could make a move for them, but Howard would be on him before he could use the keys. Silence permeated the station, and he felt his heart thudding in his chest.

Something vibrated in his pocket, and then Dan's cellphone began to ring.

Shit, he thought.

The tone echoed through the locker room and beyond, betraying any cover he may have had. He slipped the phone out of his pocket, hitting the silent button and looking at the faceplate.

It was Howard placing the call.

The footsteps in the hallway resumed, this time headed right for the locker room.

"Dan?" Howard's voice echoed from the hallway.

Dan had slipped to the end of the lockers to the right of the entrance, wedging himself between the shelf and the wall. Howard had entered the doorway, and was now only ten feet away. Dan heard the sound of fabric creasing as the officer bent down to pick something up off the ground. *He must have found my cellphone*, he thought. It was a last resort. Perhaps if the officer found the phone, he'd think it had been left there.

"I know you're in here, Dan."

No such luck.

Dan tightened his grip on the baton, holding the base in the crook of his elbow, clinging desperately to the smooth black handle. He looked across the room. A single stall and a urinal were in the corner opposite him. Next to them was a small shower, the curtain drawn. A single wooden bench stood in the middle of the room. There were only a few places for Howard to check. Soon after he stepped into the room, Dan's hiding place would be revealed.

"I don't have time for this shit," Howard yelled. He hit the side of the lockers, rattling the contents, sending vibrations through to the other end and into Dan's cheek. "I tried to do you a favor, Dan, you know? For old time's sake."

Dan clenched his teeth, felt his body tighten. Howard took a few steps forward. He entered the room.

"I even found your ungrateful daughter."

Dan had had enough.

He leapt from his hiding spot toward the senior officer, swinging the baton sideways with all of his might. Howard turned in anticipation, blocking the blow with his left forearm, and then countered with a blow from his right fist. The punch connected with Dan's ribcage, and he sprawled to the floor next to the wooden bench. He rolled underneath it to the other side, shards of pain running up his side like glass.

Howard grabbed at the underside of the bench, lifting it upwards and into the air. It collapsed on its side, striking Dan on the way down. The officer's biceps rippled under his shirt, his face twisted in anger.

"Am I going to have to kill you myself?" he asked.

Dan glared at him from the floor, still clutching the baton. His back was pressed against the lockers, and pain shot through his body. Howard took a step towards him, straddling the overturned bench.

"Why are you doing this?" Dan wheezed.

"You've done this to yourselves! Every last one of you!" Howard screamed. "You deserve it!"

"You're not making sense. What is it that we've done?"

Howard grunted, and then reached down to grab him. Dan swung the baton forward, connecting with Howard's knee. Howard cried out in pain, doubling over as his leg caved inwards.

"Motherfucker!"

Dan forced himself to stand, heading around the bench and towards the exit. He heard Quinn screaming his name from down the hall.

"I'm coming!" he shouted.

He limped ahead, approaching the doorway. Behind him, Howard yelled in pain. Dan was at the doorway now, and he reached behind him to pull the door shut. *I just might make it out of this alive*, he thought.

The door started to swing closed, then stopped with a dull thud as it struck something behind him. *Shit*.

A pair of hands grabbed Dan's shoulders, whipping him around and throwing him across the room. Dan landed on his knees, facing the shower. Howard was behind him, pulling the curtain open and forcing his head inside. He heard the officer hit the lever, heard the brief pause of water traveling through the pipe, and then felt cold water cascading out of the showerhead and onto his face.

Dan gasped for breath, liquid running up his nose and down his windpipe. Howard pushed him in further, grinding his face against the cement floor and drain, and the water started to puddle. He closed his eyes and pictured Julie's face smiling down at him. Her lips were a soft pink, her eyes a radiant blue.

Is this how I'm going to die?

He struggled for what seemed like an eternity, arms flailing backwards, striking at Howard's legs. The man was twice the size that he was. He was hopelessly outmatched. In the background, over the roar of the water, a noise drew him back from the depths. His daughter was still yelling his name.

Dan pictured Quinn on her own, fighting off a slew of the creatures — succumbing to a fate worse than his own. He felt his eyes well up and tear, mixing with the water that would soon drown him, and he propelled his arms backward one last time.

Without warning, Howard's hands retracted

and he was free. Dan rolled to the side, out of the shower, spitting and coughing. His hair was matted across his face, his vision blurry. He wiped the water from his eyes, trying to ascertain what had happened.

Why did he let me go?

Three large shapes stood in the room. Dan squinted, discerning Howard's figure among them. The other two shapes were grabbing at the senior officer, and the man had begun to scream.

Dan slid along the back wall, his vision returning.

Attacking Howard were two of the creatures.

The things tore at Howard's chest, ripping off shreds of shirt and skin. The officer was bleeding from a wound in his back, and his face was a mess of blood and fear.

Dan ran—past the creatures, past his former friend, out the door. The things paused as he flew by, but neither made a grab for him. Apparently, Howard was keeping them occupied.

He slammed the locker room door shut and held the knob. From inside, he heard Howard shrieking in pain.

Dan reached for his keys, fumbling for the one that fit the locker room door. When he found it, he inserted it into the keyhole, just as the knob started to turn.

"Dan!" a voice hissed through the door.

He stared for a moment. Howard must have somehow made it across the room, making one last play for the exit. Dan clutched the knob, listening to the sound of nails clawing at the door. He wondered briefly if the fingers belonged to the officer, or the creatures—or both.

From down the hall, his daughter was yelling his name.

Dan let go of the doorknob and started down the corridor towards the jail cell, leaving the door locked behind him.

Howard felt searing pain hit his abdomen, and then his vision blurred. He struggled to stay on his feet, but the creatures pulled him down to the floor.

This isn't supposed to happen, he screamed inside. *I'm supposed to survive.*

He replayed the last few minutes in his mind, trying to figure out where it had all gone wrong. The creatures had come at him from the main office down the hall. He'd heard a crash—had seen them break through the door.

But I secured this building myself! Dan would have come in through the front entrance—not the office. This place was sealed tight!

One of the things gouged his throat, and he gasped for air.

How the fuck had they gotten in? Did someone let them inside?

Howard struggled to break free, but the

creatures had him locked in their grip. His stomach felt hot and wet. He looked down in horror to find it had been ripped open. His intestines spilled from his gut, and he collapsed to the ground. He felt his strength start to fade.

The Agent leaders, he thought. *Would they have betrayed me?* They'd told him to return to the station. They'd known he would be here.

His memory flitted back to one of his first conversations with them, almost six years ago. The words came slowly, and he fought to remember through the pain.

"Each one of you has a purpose. To ensure that the plan is successful, you must do what is instructed of you. Nothing more."

Maybe his purpose had been served.

He felt his phone buzz in his pocket. They must be calling—checking in on him. *Making sure I'm dead...*

The warm feeling in his stomach grew cold, and Howard felt his consciousness start to slip. *How could they do this to me?*

"I did everything you asked," he whispered.

The creatures looked up at him, their eyes rabid, and then continued to tear him apart.

18

THREE DAYS HAD PASSED SINCE Julie's death.

Quinn lay curled up in a ball at Dan's feet. Although the house had two bedrooms, she refused to sleep in them. She'd insisted on sleeping on the living room floor, in the center of the house, just a few feet from her father.

Dan smiled grimly at her, watching her chest rise and fall. In the distance, he heard a long scream — whether it was from a human or one of the creatures, he wasn't sure. He stared across the room, to a pile of guns and ammunition that he had raided from the police station. It was nighttime, and he didn't dare go outside to investigate. Even in the daytime, such firepower did little to quell his nerves.

It had been Quinn's suggestion to stay here — and in hindsight, a damn good one.

Howard's home was equipped with steel doors on either side. Each had a quarter-inch metal bar that fit snugly into threaded supports along the frame. The windows contained thick metal borders, and each was made of bulletproof glass. The officer had stockpiled food throughout the house. The second bedroom contained three shelves full of dry goods, and the basement contained several freezers and refrigerators. The man had been prepared for what happened.

Since arriving, Dan had rummaged through the whole house, searching for clues as to what was happening. In the process, he had uncovered several garbage bags full of unused groceries in the trashcan out back. He had quickly identified a pattern.

All the new food had been purchased in the last two weeks. Everything else had been discarded.

Whatever was happening to St. Matthews seemed to be connected to the food and water supply. So far, Dan and Quinn hadn't been affected, but he wondered if it was a matter of time.

After their arrival, Dan had ventured outside three times, but close calls with the creatures had sent him back into the house in a hurry. He hadn't seen any signs of other survivors. The power was still on, but he wasn't sure how long it would last.

He had warned Quinn to stay away from the windows. In fact, they had kept the blinds closed throughout the house to avoid being seen by the creatures. A few times, they had watched some of the things hunting around the neighborhood, creeping in corners and sliding along walls. Dan had located a pair of binoculars in one of the drawers, and he studied the creature's movements with growing dread. If they had been infected with some disease, they showed no signs of slowing down.

Dan stood up from the couch, tiptoeing past his sleeping daughter, and parted the living room blinds. The night was still. There were only a few other houses on the street, and their lights remained off. He hadn't seen a hint of movement inside them for the past few days. He felt a pang of guilt that he hadn't checked all of them, but he couldn't bear the thought of leaving his daughter alone. He had already lost her once.

Dan thought back to what Quinn had told him— about the text message she had seen on Howard's phone.

Every last one must go.

Somewhere, others knew what was coming, as well. They had planned this. The thought made him sick to his stomach. Dan heard his daughter stir from behind him. He let go of the blinds and returned to her side.

Breakfast was jelly on bread, untoasted, and a bowl of Cheerios in milk. Dan had been avoiding the oven and the toaster, afraid that the smells might draw the attention of the creatures. The milk in Howard's fridge hadn't yet expired. It made sense to use it up. They had enough food in the house to last for a while, but he knew they couldn't stay there forever.

Sooner or later, they'd need to make their escape. They needed to get help.

Howard didn't have a phone in the house. On his few journeys out, Dan had tried to call for help — using both landlines and his cellphone. Not a single call had gone through. It was as if the whole world was dead. Try as he might, he was unable to push the awful thought from his mind.

Quinn sat across from him at the kitchen table, her mouth full of Cheerios. For a split second, Dan felt a sense of normalcy, as if today could have been any other day, as if she would soon head off to school and he to work.

"Are we going to put more food in the car, Daddy?"

"Yes, I think that's a good idea," he said.

Over the past few days, they had been transferring food from Howard's house to the Outback. Dan wanted to stock it up in case they had to leave suddenly. It was best to stay prepared.

So far, they hadn't run into any trouble, but Dan knew that their luck could change at any minute. Which was why they needed to leave St. Matthews. It wasn't safe here. He held out hope that somewhere beyond the White Mountains, things were better. That he could provide safety for his daughter.

That he could come to terms with his wife's death.

In the chaos and insanity, Dan hadn't had time to accept the reality of Julie's passing. Hell—he hadn't even been given a chance to grieve. There had been little discussion of returning home. It wasn't safe, and he didn't want Quinn to see her mother's body. The girl had been through enough.

Quinn gulped down the last bite of her Cheerios, and tilted the bowl to drink the milk from the bottom. At home, Julie would have told her to mind her manners. Now, Dan let out a guarded smile.

"Good to the last drop, huh?"

She nodded. Quinn stood, bowl in hand, and headed towards the sink. She rinsed the bowl quietly and then placed it on the counter. The spoon fell from her grip, and pinged off the basin below.

"Shhhh..." he warned.

"I know, Daddy," she returned.

She reached over to the window above the sink and parted the blinds.

"I wish we could go outside," she said. "It seems like such a beautiful day."

A ray of sunshine cleared the countertop and hit the floor. Dan followed it back up to the window, smiling.

He bolted upright in his chair.

One of the creatures was pressing its face against the pane, eyes glazed and overcast. It rapped at the glass with its knuckles, feeling for a way in. Quinn stifled a scream.

They had been discovered.

Dan crept to the living room and grabbed a pistol, then snuck over to the front blinds. He peered outside, looking for signs of movement. The road was empty, the houses across the street undisturbed. The Outback sat in the driveway. There was no sign of the thing from the backyard.

But he was sure it would make its way around front eventually.

Hopefully, it would lose interest and leave. The last thing he wanted was for it to draw others.

Quinn stood behind him, holding the back of his shirt.

"I'm sorry, Daddy," she whispered.

"It's not your fault, Quinn," he said.

And he meant it. None of it was. Not one single thing.

"Why don't you get the cooler ready? Pack it as full as you can," he instructed, hoping to keep her busy. "And bring it back to the living room. Stay clear of the blinds."

She nodded and started upstairs. Dan followed the windows one by one to the back of the house, scanning for the intruder. He finally found it, hovering by the side of the house. It looked up at him through the glass, seeming to sense his presence. Its teeth were caked with yellow and red, its skin a dull gray. The creatures were changing.

It seemed like they were growing more grotesque by the day. The thing reached up towards him and groped at the window. He dropped the blinds. With only one creature outside, they should still be safe. They'd wait it out until the thing left. It shouldn't be able to get inside.

He heard a bang from upstairs.

"Are you all right up there?" he called.

"Yes, Dad. I'm almost done."

He made his way back to the living room. A black tote bag lay on the floor next to the weapons. He filled it with as much as he could carry: ammunition, guns, and batons, as well as a bulletproof vest. When he finished, he lifted the bag and deposited it near the front door. It was best to be prepared. He returned to the windows.

This time Dan did a double take. A horde of creatures was making its way down the road, headed in their direction. Arms and legs swayed back and forth, heads bobbed, and limbs tangled as they moved in one mass. Although he was unable to count them all, he guessed there were at least twenty of the things.

He sucked in a breath, envisioning their lives in the days to come. They could hide in the house for a while, living off the food that Howard had left. Wait for help to arrive. But what if the creatures kept coming, and what if they found a way in? And more importantly, what if no help came? Try as he might, Dan couldn't help but envision the house as their tomb.

He couldn't allow that to happen.

He needed to get his daughter to safety, no matter what it took. This might be their last chance to escape St. Matthews.

"Quinn, it's time!" he yelled, trying his best to sound calm.

"Coming!"

She bounded down the stairs, the cooler swinging in front of her.

"What are you looking at? What do you see, Dad?" she asked, inching closer.

"Listen, Quinn. I'm going to need your help here. We need to move fast," he began. She started to shake. He locked eyes with her. "When I open this door, I need you to get to the car and get inside. Don't look around—just lock the doors. I'll be right behind you."

"Dad, I'm scared!"

"We're going to get out of here, and we're going to get help," he assured her.

She clung on to his shirt, crying. His heart felt like a stone in his chest. She looked into his eyes and nodded. Dan moved towards the front door, carrying the tote bag. He lifted the metal rod from the holders and unlocked it. Through the screen, he could see the swarm of creatures getting closer.

"Oh my God…" Quinn whispered.

"Don't look. When I open the door, run straight to the car."

He handed her the key, and gave her one last look before pushing open the screen door. His daughter took off in front of him. Dan threw the tote bag into the front yard, and retrieved the pistol from the floor. He then slammed the door shut behind him and stepped outside.

Quinn was almost at the car already, her legs pumping against the walkway. She carried the cooler in front of her. She was at the passenger's side door now, unlocking the vehicle. The creatures broke into a run, fanning out across the street. Dan grabbed the weapons bag and began to sprint. Adrenaline coursed through his arms, and he held the pistol sideways at the approaching mob.

The tote bag tangled in something, and he stopped short, losing his grip. He glanced behind him. The creature from the backyard had snagged it, and the thing dove into him, clawing at his leg, pulling him onto the grass. Dan yelled in surprise, and the pistol he was holding flew from his hands.

"Daddy!"

Quinn had opened the car door, but instead of getting inside, she stood next to it and yelled his name.

"Get in and lock the doors!" he cried out.

The creature locked its grip on his pants, and he felt nails dig into his pants. He kicked backwards at it. He was pinned. Quinn got back in the car and shut the door behind her.

Footsteps hit the grass around him. The others had entered the property, and he heard them groaning in unison. He pushed up from the ground, trying to shake the thing loose. The creature clung on to his back, unrelenting.

The car horn sounded.

Dan looked to his left. A few of the creatures moved towards the vehicle.

"Quinn—no! Don't draw their attention!"

He wrenched his back to the side, and the creature loosened its grasp. He swung an elbow backwards, felt the crunch of bone behind him as it connected with the thing's face. Suddenly he was free.

Dan regained his footing and stumbled toward the car. Several other creatures lunged in his direction, but he weaved from side to side, dodging them.

Finally he reached the driver's side door. Quinn stopped hitting the horn, and she threw open the door to allow him access. He jumped inside.

Quinn had already started the engine. Dan threw the vehicle into reverse and careened out of the driveway, the car door still swinging open behind him.

19

Dan maneuvered the Outback through St. Matthews, the streets lifeless and empty. Even in the daylight, porch lights still burned in front of some of the houses. Doors were left open; windows were smashed. Quinn sat upright in the passenger seat next to him biting her nails.

They passed by a carcass on the side of the road. A few birds picked at the remains, and then scattered at the sight of the approaching car. Farther ahead, a creature emerged from a driveway, holding a fistful of hair. Quinn stared, unable to look away.

"Close your eyes," he said, knowing she wouldn't.

Dan continued driving toward the outskirts of town. The houses grew more infrequent. He looked down at the gas gauge, which showed that the tank was half empty. They would need more than that to have a fighting chance. There was a gas station about a mile up the road — the last one in town before heading into the White Mountains.

He saw it now, up ahead, and he pulled into

the parking lot next to the pumps, hoping they were still operational. He drew his pistol and left the car running. Although he had lost the tote bag at the house, he had hidden one gun in the car. *Thank God*, he thought.

The gas station was deserted. The front windows had been smashed, and items of food and clothing were strewn across the front entrance. Dan scanned in all directions, finding nothing. He opened the car door, gripping the weapon, and popped the gas tank.

The pumps appeared functional—their lights indicated the price of gas, and options for payment. Dan pulled his wallet out and removed his debit card. He chuckled slightly. Even at the end of existence, the oil companies were still making out like bandits. He contemplated going inside to search for supplies, but decided against it. He had risked enough. They needed to get as far away from St. Matthews as possible.

Dan topped off the tank, and then opened the trunk, where he kept a gas can. He filled it to the top, replaced the spout cap, and put it back in the vehicle. He got back into the car and locked the door.

"Daddy?"

"Yes, honey?"

"Where are we going to go?"

"Away from here. Things will be better once we get out of town," he said.

"Do you promise?" Quinn looked at him, her eyes wide.

"I promise."

Dan pulled out from the gas station and into the road. Up ahead, Route 191 wound up into the mountains, providing a bridge to the outside world. He hit the gas and felt the car accelerate, then rolled his window down, letting in the fresh morning air.

They have to get better, he told himself. They sure as hell couldn't get any worse.

TO BE CONTINUED

Contamination 1: The Onset follows another group of survivors as they struggle to escape the chaos…and to discover the truth about what is happening.

Dan and Quinn return in Contamination 2: Crossroads!

****REVIEWS****

If you enjoyed CONTAMINATION: BOOK ZERO, PLEASE leave a review, as this would be a HUGE help in allowing others to discover my works and will allow me to keep doing what I love most: writing!

Take care and happy reading!

-Tyler

Want to know when the next book is coming out?
Sign up for NEW RELEASE ALERTS
and get a FREE STORY!
http://eepurl.com/qy_SH

ABOUT THE AUTHOR

T.W. Piperbrook was born and raised in Connecticut, where he can still be found today. He is the author of the **CONTAMINATION** series, the **OUTAGE** series, and the co-author of **THE LAST SURVIVORS**.

He lives with his wife, a son, and the spirit of his Boston Terrier, Ricky.

LIKE him on Facebook at: www.facebook.com/twpiperbrook

READ ON FOR A PREVIEW OF CONTAMINATION 1: THE ONSET!

BOOK ONE: THE ONSET

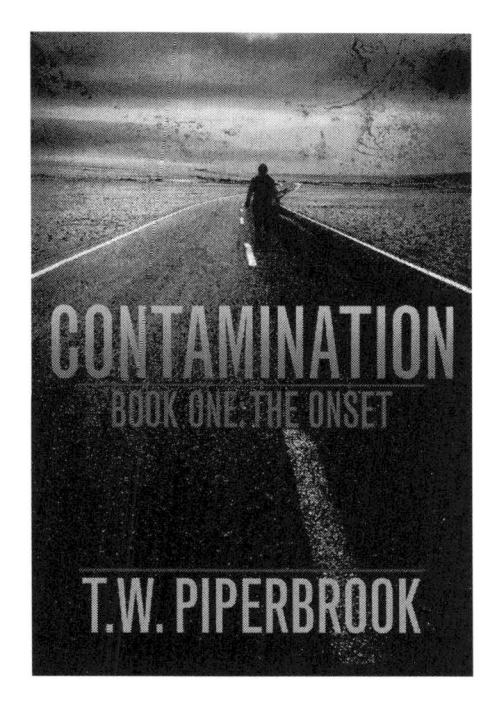

DEDICATION

Dedicated to CED, for your never-ending support, and to CBA for setting this thing into motion.

PART ONE
EXODUS

1

White Mist, New Mexico
Population: 1

SURROUNDED BY WHIPPING SAND AND dust, the brown sign stood resilient at the town's perimeter. Sam Cook could still make out the faded sticker that had been placed over the single numeric digit on its face, even though it had been a few years. That was how the DOT amended things these days. If a change were small enough, a patch would suffice to update the information.

He could've requested a new sign—hell, he was now the only resident of the town. But the thin border around the number reminded him of the sign's previous digit. It was one he did not want to forget.

He imagined a line that should have been placed underneath:
White Mist, New Mexico
Former Population: 3.

Sam had only lived in town with his wife and daughter for two years before the tragedy had occurred. Together, they'd rebuilt the historic log cabin store, turning it into a small-scale tourist attraction. Purchasing the town had been a lifelong dream, and they'd poured all their efforts into it.

Because the White Mist store contained a post office, it qualified for its own zip code. Several families had once resided there, but they'd long since relocated. The previous owners were an elderly couple from Iowa. They'd decided to sell the property when the upkeep became too much to handle.

Sam's family had spent long hours renovating the property, and he was proud of what they had accomplished. He liked to think that after a few short years, the White Mist Trading Post had become not only a pit stop for gas and beverages, but a piece of history and a symbol of the American West.

A bit of a stretch, perhaps. But now the store was all he had.

The shelves were adorned with a variety of commemorative merchandise: White Mist shirts, mugs, key chains, and hats. It didn't cost much to produce them, and they helped tremendously in keeping the place afloat and in keeping his family clothed and fed.

Of course, now there was only one mouth to feed.

At the moment, the store was empty. Sam wiped a trickle of sweat from his brow and paused. In front of him was a half-empty shelf of dried noodles. On the floor was a case of replenishments. He needed a break.

He moved towards the screen door at the entrance, listening to the floor squeak underneath him. The door seemed ready to expire; it creaked on its hinges, begging for relief. The place needed work. He tried his best to keep it up, but there was only so much he could do alone.

He surveyed the empty parking lot in front of him. Beyond it was an equally deserted portion of I-40. The southwestern desert stretched endlessly for miles, composed of scorching, earthy landscape, with occasional patches of green that helped offset the brown scenery. In the distance, a few mountains rose skyward.

On the horizon, he saw what looked like a tractor-trailer barreling down the interstate. The setting sun glinted off its hood, capturing the last glimmers of daylight in its grill. Overhead, a lone hawk circled, probably already watching its unsuspecting prey.

The truck looked like it was slowing down. Sam used the top of his sleeve to wipe another bead of perspiration from his forehead, unknowingly smearing a line of dirt in a half-circle. He went inside.

He heard the driver pumping the brakes, then the truck tires crunching to a halt. Through the screen windows of the store, he saw the words 'All-American Beef' emblazoned on the side. The driver's window was rolled all the way up, and Sam was unable to see through the tinted glass.

A sudden fear coursed through his body, making him shiver.

"What the hell?" he muttered to himself. "It's gotta be like ninety-eight degrees out."

Sam had grown accustomed to talking to himself. It felt good to keep a monologue going, especially when no one else was there to judge or listen. In this case, however, the one-sided conversation was an attempt to calm his nerves.

What was he afraid of? Trucks came through White Mist all day long, filling up on diesel gasoline, taking a break from the open road.

But this one seemed different.

Outside, the hawk swooped lazily. It had either lost sight of its target, or it was still toying with it. The truck sat in silence. There was no sign of movement from the driver.

Sam glanced over at the floor to the case of noodles. For some reason, he felt like he should continue to unpack it — to act as natural as possible. But that would leave him unprepared. For what, he wasn't sure.

Beneath the cash register, strapped underneath the shelf, he kept a loaded rifle. It had been there so long he imagined it was covered with a layer of dust — hell, he wasn't even sure it worked anymore. He mentally traced the steps from where he stood to the cash register.

Six or seven steps. That's what he'd need to reach the counter. Sam stood at six-foot-one inches and weighed a hundred and eighty pounds. He had long strides.

"This is ridiculous." He forced a smile. "I'm being ridiculous."

As if in response, the truck door swung open with a groan, and a short man with a baseball cap hopped out into the parking lot. Sam jumped slightly.

"Whew!" the trucker yelled to no one in particular. "It's damn hot out today!"

Sam breathed a sigh of relief. He considered going out to greet the customer. Instead, he stuck to the noodles.

The trucker bounded through the door with a flurry of conversation. Sam imagined the man had been talking the entire trip, with or without an audience.

"Howdy, sir! I need me a drink. It's hot as blazes out there!"

"Welcome to White Mist!" Sam welcomed him. "The cooler is to the left. Before you ask, yes — I am the population of one."

"I kinda figured that!" the guy chuckled. "But I'm sure you get that question all the time."

"You wouldn't believe it!" Sam groaned. In truth, he liked the casual banter, the harmless jokes. It helped him take his mind off other, more serious things.

The trucker brought his purchase to the register and paid in cash. Sam counted back the change and shut the drawer, watching him leave the store.

He returned to stocking the shelf, lining up the noodles next to each other.

I must be getting jittery in my old age.

Either that, or maybe the isolation was starting to manifest itself as anxiety. In any case, Sam was looking forward to closing up shop in just a few hours and heading to his trailer home next door. It had been a long day, and he could use the rest.

He didn't hear his next customer come through the door until the screen creaked on its hinges and slammed shut.

"Welcome to White Mist," Sam called out. He smiled, and then decided to add: "The best thing west of Roswell!"

He was greeted by silence. A dark figure had emerged from behind the shelf.

The man had a pale, lifeless expression. His mouth was clamped shut, and his face looked as if it had aged unnaturally, sucking his dark facial hair into the folds of his cheeks. A scar ran sideways across his throat. The skin around it appeared jagged and flaky, as if it had been picked at during the healing process.

His black eyes seemed to pierce through the storeowner.

The figure was not amused.

Sam attempted to stand, tripping over the now-empty case of noodles beside him.

The man with the scar didn't move. His eyes

flitted wildly around the store, as if someone had scooped them out of his head and had replaced them with two black marbles.

"Can I help you?" Sam attempted. His own voice sounded foreign, as if someone else had spoken the words.

The man's eyes stopped roaming. Instead of answering, he moved towards Sam, his hands raised in what appeared to be attack mode.

Sam wasn't sure of what the man's intentions were, but he wasn't going to wait around to find out.

Six or seven steps. That's what I need to reach the rifle.

Sam ran. Before he knew it, he'd travelled half the distance to the counter, and he dove to the floor and tore at the underside of the shelf, removing the rifle from its perch. His pulse thudded in his ears; his heart pounded in his chest.

A loud crash rang out from behind him, but Sam stayed low, remaining on the ground until the noise had subsided.

When it was quiet, Sam rose to his haunches and leveled the rifle over the counter, aiming at where his attacker had been.

Only the man was gone.

Two of the store's shelves had toppled completely over, spilling their contents onto the floor, and several cans and containers spun where they had landed.

The man with the scar was not among the debris.

"Jesus." Sam felt the air escape his lungs.

Was he imagining things? Losing his mind?

Either Sam was going insane—dreaming up the horrific figure and the ensuing chase—or somewhere his unknown assailant was plotting his next move.

Although a part of him preferred insanity, he was cautious enough to believe what his eyes had told him. There had definitely been another customer in the store—there had to have been. Sam pictured the man now lurking in one of the store's corners, black eyes darting wildly around the store, and shuddered. The rifle shook in his hands.

"Hey mister!" A somewhat familiar voice rang from outside. "You all right?"

Sam jumped at the sound. It took him a second to recognize the jovial tone of the previous customer. *The trucker with the baseball hat,* he thought. Through the screen of the front door, he could still make out the 'All-American Beef' logo in the parking lot. Had the trucker seen the assailant enter the store?

Sam held his breath, resisting the urge to cry out. Although his attacker must surely know where he was, he didn't want to betray his position. Just in case.

The trucker pressed his nose up to the screen

and peered inside. A look of concern crossed his face as he surveyed the scene.

"You still in there, mister?"

Get out of here! Sam wanted to scream.

The man continued to peer inside. He raised his hand above his eyes to get a better look, tilting his baseball cap upward. Sam watched in slow motion, praying he would leave.

Regardless of what was happening, one thing was clear: they were both in danger.

Before Sam could warn the man, a shadow rose up from the interior of the store, and a fist swung up and shattered the trucker's nose through the screen. Blood spurted through the meshing, spraying a red mist into the store. The customer flew backwards and landed in the dirt outside, shrieking in pain.

"Holy Jesus!" Sam cried out. His palms were soaking wet now, and his hands slipped across the rifle. He aimed towards the entrance, his hands wobbly, but the shadow moved out of view.

Sam ducked down, scanning the store for signs of activity.

The attacker was here somewhere. He must be. He felt the man's presence, could sense him watching. Sam's eyes roved the store, flitting from wall to wall. Eventually he focused on a nearby shelf unit. He heard a scraping noise from behind it, and he stared intently, waiting for a figure to pop into view.

Without warning, the shelf unit slid across

the floor toward the counter. It was filled with products, and must have weighed at least a hundred pounds. From behind it, Sam could hear the jagged breathing of the assailant.

The shelf was being pushed right at him.

Sam pulled the trigger on the rifle, firing off a round.

A can of vegetables exploded from the shelf's middle, sending pieces of wood throughout the store, but the shelf kept moving and collided with the counter.

Sam ducked, shielding his face from the debris. Merchandise toppled to the floor, rattling and spinning. The shrieking outside had stopped. He imagined the man with the baseball cap must have passed out from the pain—or worse.

Silence wove its way through the store once again.

Sam opened his eyes, rose from behind the counter. The screen door was swinging back and forth, broken off of one of its hinges. It looked like the attacker had departed through it.

Once again his assailant was a step ahead of him.

Want to read more?
CONTAMINATION 1: THE ONSET
is AVAILABLE NOW!

COMPLETE CONTAMINATION SERIES AVAILABLE NOW!

CONTAMINATION PREQUEL
CONTAMINATION 1: THE ONSET
CONTAMINATION 2: CROSSROADS
CONTAMINATION 3: WASTELAND
CONTAMINATION 4: ESCAPE
CONTAMINATION 5: SURVIVAL
CONTAMINATION 6: SANCTUARY

OTHER SERIES:

OUTAGE 1 - FREE!
OUTAGE 2: AWAKENING

THE LAST SURVIVORS (co-written w/Bobby Adair)

Contamination Book Zero
Copyright © 2012 by T. W. Piperbrook. All rights reserved.

Print Edition: May 2015

Editing: Ashley Davis
Proofreading: Linda Tooch
Cover Design: Keri Knutson
Formatting: Streetlight Graphics

For more information on the author's work, visit:
http://www.twpiperbrook.com

Thanks to my friends and family, who have supported and inspired me. Special thanks to my Aunt Gaye Hooper—a fellow dreamer.

No part of this book may be reproduced, scanned, or distributed in any printed or electronic form without permission. Please do not participate in or encourage piracy of copyrighted materials in violation of the author's rights. Thank you for respecting the hard work of this author.

The characters and events portrayed in this book are a work of fiction or are used fictitiously. Any similarity to real persons, living or dead, is coincidental and not intended by the author.

19114210R10086

Printed in Great Britain
by Amazon